# WAVES OF DESTRUCTION

The *Blenheim* had begun circling for another attack when Hamilton realized that *Rapier's* deck gun was silent. He hurried to the front of the bridge to find out what was going on. The gun crew had vanished. *And so had the gun!*

All that remained was a gaping hole in the deck plating. The blast of the bombs had wrenched the one-ton weapon from its mounting as cleanly as a dentist removing a decayed tooth from a patient's jaw.

There was no trace of sentiment in Hamilton's reaction to the tragedy. The four men of the gun crew could be replaced. But, deprived of her single anti-aircraft gun, *Rapier* was now defenseless against the renewed onslaught of the bomber. Hamilton bent over the voicepipe.

"Bring our two Vickers to the bridge, Number One. The deck gun's been knocked out. We'll have to fight it out with machineguns!"

"Captain, sir! Look at *this*!"

Hamilton spun around in response to the coxswain's incredulous shout. Good God! As if they hadn't enough to cope with already.

An enemy U-boat had surfaced. And it was steaming straight toward them with its deck guns manned and ready to open fire.

*Also by Edwyn Gray:*

**No Survivors**
**Action Atlantic**
**Tokyo Torpedo** —
**The Last Command**

# FIGHTING SUBMARINE

### EDWYN GRAY

PINNACLE BOOKS      NEW YORK

This is a work of fiction. All the characters and events portrayed in this book are fictional, and any resemblance to real people or incidents is purely coincidental.

FIGHTING SUBMARINE

*Copyright © 1978 by Edward Kaufman*

Pinnacle Books edition, published by special arrangement with Futura Publications Limited.

First printing, April 1981

ISBN: 0-523-41399-8

Cover illustration by Ed Valigursky

*Printed in the United States of America*

**PINNACLE BOOKS, INC.**
1430 Broadway
New York, New York 10018

# FIGHTING SUBMARINE

Edwyn Gray enjoys an international reputation as both a crisply exciting story-teller and a serious naval historian. Born in London "sufficiently long ago" he was educated at the Cooper's Company School and the Royal Grammar School, High Wycombe, and now lives in the Buckinghamshire village of Penn with his family "and an ever increasing number of dogs."

His first short story was published in 1952 and he has been a contributor to leading British, American and Australian magazines for over 20 years. His first full length book appeared in 1969 and his time is now equally divided between standard works on modern naval history and novels based on the war at sea—both above and below the surface.

FIGHTING SUBMARINE is the first book in the second submarine series.

# CHAPTER ONE

"I give you a toast, Sir Charles. To our two great navies. And may they always fight on the same side."

Von Hauptmann raised his glass and bowed stiffly. The *Vizeadmiral's* guest of honor would have preferred a pink gin but the *Kriegsmarine* had not, apparently, discovered the subtleties of the Royal Navy's palate. The steward, standing rigid and silent at his side, had only champagne to offer. Making the best of a bad job Rear-Admiral Sir Charles Robertson took a glass and raised it in response to the toast.

"To our two Navies, *Vizeadmiral*. And may we never fight at all."

The officers gathered in the spacious wardroom of the battle cruiser *Gneisenau* laughed politely, echoed the toast and summoned a steward to recharge their glasses. It was a warm summer's afternoon and, despite the German warship's air-conditioning system, both guests and hosts felt hot and sticky in their tight-fitting dress uniforms. Goodwill parties were all very well but there were occasions when they became tedious. Few of the junior officers had gone to bed before dawn after spending a riotous night at the Yacht Club. They were only too well aware that they had to attend the Admiral's Ball later that evening and wished that the top-brass would get it over quickly so that they could snatch a few hours of sleep before the next part of the celebrations began.

Taking Sir Charles by the arm von Hamptmann led him into one of the anterooms on the starboard side of the battle-cruiser. Shaded from the sun, its ports wide open to admit the breeze blowing in across Kiel Bay, and with a large deckhead fan stirring the turgid air, it was quiet and cool after the hubbub of the crowded wardroom.

"I see from your medal ribbons that you served in the last war, Sir Charles." Von Hauptmann walked to a steel-fronted locker, pulled down the flap and revealed his private liquor store. An expectant gleam appeared in Sir Charles's eyes as he saw the display of bottles. "Let's throw this fizzy rubbish away and have a man's drink. A pink gin for you?"

His guest nodded and visibly mellowed as the *Vizeadmiral* passed him the glass. Von Hauptmann poured himself a small measure of kummel.

"I was with the Scouting Force at the Horn's Reef," he continued. "I have never understood how your Admiral Jellicoe let us escape. It was a miracle none of us had dared hope for."

Robertson nodded. The Germans always referred to the battle as Horn's Reef. To the British it was better known as Jutland.

"I was there too. With Beatty's battle-cruisers. You gave us a real hammering and no mistake. We were lucky to turn the tables on you and lead you into the arms of the Grand Fleet."

*"Ach so,"* von Hauptmann agreed. "I thought we were done for when we saw Jellicoe's battleships." He sighed at the memory. "It was a great day. And it ended as none of us had expected."

The British admiral reached for the gin bottle which von Hauptmann had thoughtfully placed on the table. He looked across at his host. On May 31, 1916, they had been facing each other across the gray wastes of the North Sea, engaged in a fight to the death. Who would have imagined then that, twenty years later, they would be sharing drinks on board a *Kriegsmarine* flagship and reminiscing like old shipmates?

"It was an unnecessary battle," the *Vizeadmiral* continued. "The Royal Navy should have done what we had always expected it to do. You could have won the war in a single day."

"And what was that?"

"To—how do you say?—Copenhagen the German fleet before war was officially declared."

Robertson laughed. "My dear Admiral, you really should know that the British Navy doesn't do such things. It's not cricket."

"But your Admiral Nelson did," von Hauptmann pointed out. "And so did the Japanese when they attacked Port Arthur in '04. If you can gain the advantage of surprise nothing can defeat a pre-emptive strike. Believe me, Sir Charles, had the Royal Navy struck at the German Navy in July, 1914, there would have been no war. Without a fleet the Kaiser was powerless."

Despite von Hauptmann's geniality and the soothing effect of the gin Rear-Admiral Robertson was feeling uncomfortable. Although he fervently believed that war between Germany and Britain was impossible, or at worst unthinkable, he was averse to discussing tactics with a potential enemy. Perhaps the *Vizeadmiral* knew something of the Admiralty's war plans of which he was unaware.

Or perhaps he was giving his guest a subtle warning of Germany's own aggressive intentions. He was still searching for a diplomatic reply when a tall sour-faced officer entered the anteroom, hesitated as if unwilling to interrupt a private conversation between senior officers, and then politely clicked his heels and bowed.

Von Hauptmann rose to his feet to effect the necessary introductions. "May I present *Kapitan zur See* Mikel, Sir Charles. He has just been appointed to command of our new *panzerschiffe Koenig*."*

The *kapitan* bowed again and took Robertson's hand in a cold friendless clasp.

"An honor, *Herr* Admiral." Somehow he made the compliment sound like a sneer. "I hope you will pay my ship a visit before you leave Kiel."

"Sir Charles and I were discussing old times," von Hauptmann interrupted.

"You were at Horn's Reef as well, were you not *Herr Kapitan?*"

"*Ja,* that is so. I was a cadet on *Derfflinger*." He held up his left hand to show three missing fingers. "I still have this reminder of a British shell. I was only eighteen years old at the time. My consolation is that we won the battle."

Robertson ignored the boast. "We were talking

*\*Panzerschiffe*=armored ship. Outside Germany these heavily armed vessels were known as pocket battleships.

3

about Nelson at Copenhagen," he said, to change the subject. "I was just reassuring the *Vizeadmiral* that the British Navy does not do that sort of thing these days."

"Only because your new generation has no guts," Mikel retorted aggressively. "You British have grown soft and decadent. Just look at the debate at your Oxford University.* Can you imagine any German student voting not to fight for the Fatherland?"

"I wouldn't read too much into that, if I were you, *Herr Kapitan,*" Robertson said quietly. "If it ever comes to war, and God forbid that it does, I think they'll surprise quite a few people."

*Kapitan* Mikel shrugged. "I doubt it, sir. In fact I doubt if there is a single officer in the Royal Navy under the age of forty who would obey an order such as Nelson issued at Copenhagen. And, even if they did, I can assure you that the German Navy is in no danger of being caught like the Danish fleet. We are constantly on the alert. Our sailors and our organization are the finest in the world. You can take my word, Sir Charles. Any attempt to Copenhagen the *Kriegsmarine* will be doomed to ignominious failure!"

"Buelk Point—bearing Green Nine Zero, sir!"

Lieutenant Commander Cavendish had selected the low headland thrusting into the western fringe of Kiel Bay as his fix for the starting point of the final approach several days earlier. And leaning over the voicepipe to the control room he relayed his orders with the same casual calm he used for the submarine's routine diving exercises in Stoke's Bay.

"Take her down to periscope depth, Number One."

Cavendish did not believe in diving on the klaxon except in dire emergency. And despite the presence of a Blohm & Voss float-plane circling over Labö he saw no reason to hurry.

"Clutches out—switches on. Group up. Full ahead both." Hamilton, the submarine's first lieutenant, put

---

*Mikel was referring to the notorious Oxford Union debate when a motion to "fight for King and country" was narrowly defeated by the undergraduates.

4

the telephone link to the engine room on its hook and turned to the two coxswains at the hydroplane controls and Scruer, the "outside" ERA,* at the main blowing panel. "Open main vents. Planes hard a'dive!"

"All hands clear the bridge!"

The skipper's order to the men still on deck coincided with the muffled clang of the vents opening. Almost simultaneously the bellowing roar of sea water flooding into the empty ballast tanks drowned every other sound. Cavendish waited beside the conning-tower's upper hatch as the lookouts dropped through the oval aperture and slid down the ladder. No one seemed to hurry but it took less than ten seconds to clear the bridge and, as he swung his legs into the hatch, he took one last quick survey of the horizon before closing the heavy counter-weighted hatch cover and pulling the clips.

*HMS Surge* furrowed her bows into the foaming sea like a ploughshare vanishing beneath the soil. In due course she would reap the fruits of her labors in a harvest of death. The lathered water closed over her rust-streaked hull and, by the time her skipper had descended through the lower hatch and slid down into the control room, only her conning-tower remained above the surface. And in another ten seconds that, too, had disappeared.

"Fifteen feet . . . twenty feet . . ."

Coxswain Hawkins called off the depth-gauge readings while his companion, Jock Stewart, the second coxswain, kept a watchful eye on the bubble of the inclinometer to check the angle of dive.

"Twenty-five feet."

"Stand by," Hamilton warned from his position behind the main blowing panel. He watched the long red needle of the depth-gauge swing toward the 30 feet calibration. "Up helm!"

Stewart turned the wheel controlling the fore-planes and the submarine's bows came up gently as the diving angle eased. Hawkins's eyes did not waver from the dial of the depth-gauge. It was his job to level the subma-

*Engine-room artificer.

5

rine off at the required depth by means of the aft
planes. As the bows rose he turned his wheel to bring
the boat into a horizontal position. It was a task requir-
ing long experience and delicate judgement. And the
two coxswains sensed rather than saw the amount of
correction needed.

"Catch the trim, Number One!"

Hamilton swore softly under his breath. The submarine's trim had been perfect when they sailed from
Rosyth but a layer of fresh water, a not uncommon
phenomenon in the Baltic, was upsetting his calculations.

"Flood 1 and 2 compensating tanks."

Scruer pulled down the levers to pump water ballast
into the two forward compensating tanks and watched
the inclinometer level off. The water passing along the
narrow pipelines made a gurgling noise and the men on
duty in the control room exchanged grins as the inevi-
table humorist murmured, "Pardon me. Must have
been something I ate."

"Up periscope!"

Leading Seaman Smith pushed the control lever and
the bronze search periscope rose from its greased well
in the floor. Cavendish gripped the guide handles,
pushed his face against the eye-piece, and carried out a
quick 360° check of the surface situation. Satisfied that
they were in no imminent danger of collision he swung
the lens toward a small black and white checkered
lighthouse south of Buelk Point, read off the bearing
from the annular scale just above the eye-piece and
stepped back.

"Down periscope."

Moving to the chart table he stared down at the
chart for a few moments and then glanced at the gyro
repeater.

"Steer 1-9-0, helmsman." He picked up the telephone. "Motor room? Group down. Half ahead both."

Conserving electric power was a vital test of a submarine skipper's skill. The endurance of the electric
motors used for underwater running was limited by the
capacity of the batteries and, despite each battery con-
taining 168 "wet" cells weighing half a ton apiece, they

6

could supply power for only one hour at a maximum speed of 9 knots. Handled gently though, and holding a crawling speed of 2 knots, they could last out for a day and a half. And the amp-hour reserves in the batteries was always foremost in the mind of an experienced submarine captain.

"Should be there in approximately two hours, Number One," Cavendish said casually as he turned away from the chart and joined Hamilton at the main blowing panel.

"You still intend to go through with it then, sir?"

The lieutenant commander shrugged. "Why not? These bloody regattas always bore the arse off me. We need to do something to show 'em the Royal Navy's not asleep on the job."

"May I have a word with you in private, sir?" Hamilton asked.

It had seemed one hell of a good joke when the skipper first laid out his plans in the depot ship's wardroom after a good dinner and a convivial evening in the bar. But in the cold clear light of morning Hamilton could foresee the fearful consequences of the escapade. The Germans were not renowned for their sense of humor and it might give them just what they wanted—a justifiable pretext for war!

"Only a few minutes, Number One. The approach run will be tricky. Go to the wardroom and wait for me." Cavendish clicked his fingers. "Up periscope."

Bending forward he caught the handles of the 'scope as the tube rose from its well. His body straightened slightly but he was still in a crouched position as it broke surface. "Stop!"

Smith brought the lever to neutral. Just a few bare inches of stalk showed above the waves and the spray threw droplets of water over the tilted glass of the quick-draining lens. Visibility was not vitally important, however, and, disregarding the spray, Cavendish swung the objective lens to starboard to locate his next fix. The sewage outfall pipe jutted thirty yards into the bay to clear the effluent from the coast and, focusing on the mouth of the pipe, he took a reading from the scale

7

and called it off to Lieutenant Markham, the Third Officer and Navigator.

"Sewage pipe bearing 0-4-0, pilot."

"0-4-0, sir."

The periscope turned to the left as Cavendish searched down the shore on the other side of the bay for a cross-bearing. The mast of the radio repeater station at Labö centered in the eye-piece.

"Labö wireless beacon bearing 3-3-7. Down periscope."

The navigation officer measured off the angle and sliced a thin pencil line across the chart to intersect a similar line which he had traced on the bearing of the sewage pipe. He moved to one side as Cavendish bent across the chart and tilted the lamp slightly to illuminate the point where the two lines crossed. There was shoaling water just under a mile ahead. But they should have a clear run for the next fifteen minutes.

"Alter course to 1-9-3," he instructed the helmsman. *Surge* was closing toward the Labö side of the bay and it was vital to keep to the center channel so that he had freedom of maneuver if they were spotted.

"1-9-3, sir."

Cavendish waited until the gyro repeater had settled itself on 1-9-3 and then turned to the navigation officer.

"Take over the Watch while I find out what's bothering Hamilton, Mr. Markham. Maintain course and speed. And keep on top of the hydrophone operators. We're running shallow and I don't want a collision. If they pick up any HE steer away and don't resume course until we're safely clear. If necessary flood down and kill the motors. But remember—we've only got twenty feet of water under the keel. So if you have to go deeper use the emergency tanks and don't try diving on the 'planes. We'd be bloody unpopular with everyone if we got ourselves stuck on the bottom."

Markham grinned. He knew what Cavendish meant. As navigator he had seen the submarine's sailing orders. And running submerged inside German territorial waters certainly wasn't one of them.

"Understood, sir."

8

"Good. And don't use the periscope. This is an operational run. Let's see how good we are." Cavendish turned away, glanced at the dials and warning lights to reassure himself that *Surge* was secure and then, ducking through the oval hatch in No. 4 watertight bulkhead, he made his way down the narrow companionway to the privacy of the submarine's wardroom.

Lieutenant Commander Gerald Cavendish RN had been born with the proverbial silver spoon in his mouth. Coming from an old naval family his future career was assured, and, backed by the fortune his father, Admiral George Cavendish, had obtained by prudently marrying an American heiress shortly before the 1914–18 War, he was never bothered by shortage of money. In the eyes of his superiors he was destined for high places. Flag rank certainly—perhaps even a seat on the Board in due course—although, as they agreed over their port, the young devil would have to learn to curb his impetuosity first. It was an opinion not altogether shared by his colleagues. And even his friends were forced to admit that he owed his recent promotion to three-ring status as much to his exploits on the polo field and his connections in the right places as to his contribution to the efficiency and discipline of the Royal Navy.

In the eyes of the Lower Deck, however, he was little less than a god. The ordinary British sailor has, from time immemorial, adored the eccentric and Cavendish's escapades were always the center of attention. His successes with his supercharged Alvis at Brooklands—where he held the class lap record on the outer circuit—were followed just as closely as the conspicuous lack of success shown by his racehorse Yellow Admiral. And his succession of scandalous affairs with every eligible society beauty known to the gossip columnists added zest and color to the drabness of their gray mess-deck world.

Cavendish's adventures were seized upon, embroidered, and given a dimension that soon set him

9

apart from his fellow officers and imbued him with the aura of a living legend. And the men who served under him, in typical Royal Navy fashion, basked in the reflected glory of their skipper's notoriety.

As he sat waiting on the leather bench that ran along the curved starboard bulkhead of the wardroom, Lieutenant Hamilton decided that he had few feelings either way about his skipper. As a career officer and an upper-yardman* he was not given to hero worship. And he was dourly unimpressed by money or social position. He'd found Gerry Cavendish an efficient skipper, a good shipmate, and a natural-born leader. And that was all he asked of a fellow officer.

Only one thing marred the relationship—Cavendish's fervent admiration of Nazi Germany. Not that he was alone in his views. Many naval officers found themselves appreciating the healthy efficiency of Hitler's Third Reich, although, with the naïvety of the professional seamen, few bothered to look below the shiny skin of the apple at the rottenness inside. Cavendish, however, was louder in his enthusiasm for the new Germany than most, and as several branches of his family had married into the Prussian and Bavarian aristocracy Germany was like a second home to him. He spoke the language perfectly, visited the mountains every year for the winter sports, and spent most summers, naval duties permitting, shooting and climbing with his friends and relatives.

Had Hamilton not been fair-minded, he might have held all this against his skipper. But he knew his commanding officer well enough to realize that, for all his outer show, Cavendish was a patriot. And, if the crunch ever came, he would fight the Germans just as fervently as he now praised them.

"Well, Nick, what's this all about?"

Cavendish threw his cap onto the table and settled down in the wardroom's only armchair so that he was facing his companion. The lieutenant commander was barely thirty years old and his unruly blond hair and

*Royal Navy slang for a commissioned officer promoted from the lower-deck.

cool blue eyes gave him the appearance of a handsome Nordic god.

"Are you still going through with this damn fool scheme of yours?" Hamilton asked bluntly.

"Why not?" Cavendish grinned with anticipation. "I've bet Max Müller of the *Gneisenau* that I can make the *Kriegsmarine* sit up and I don't see why I should lose money just because you've got cold feet."

"Not cold feet, sir. More a matter of cold logic. There'll be all hell let loose if you're serious about the plan."

"Rubbish, Number One."

Hamilton paused for a moment as if making up his mind what he should do next. He decided he had to take the plunge regardless of consequences.

"I'm sorry, sir, but in my view you are giving an illegal order. And, as such, I have the right to refuse to obey."

"You have no such bloody right, Lieutenant!" The muscles of Cavendish's jaw tightened and his normally languid eyes hardened. His customary nonchalance had gone and Hamilton was disconcerted by the determination he could read in the skipper's face. "You're always lecturing me about going by the book, Number One. Well, I suggest you read Paragraph 8 of KR and AI!"* Striding to the bookshelf immediately above Hamilton's head, he pulled down the blue-covered book, opened it at page two and read: *"If an officer should receive from his superior an order which he deems at variance with his obedience to any article in these regulations . . . he is to represent verbally such contrariety to the officer from when he receives it; and if after such representation that officer shall still direct him to obey the order, he is to do so; but if he thinks it necessary, he may report the circumstances as the case may require through his captain to his commander-in-chief or to the admiralty."* He slammed the book shut. "Well *I'm* directing you to obey my orders, Mr. Hamilton. And you can complain to who the hell you like *afterwards*. Do I make myself clear?"

*King's Regulations and Admiralty Instructions.

"Perfectly—and don't think I won't." Hamilton's ruffled temper quickly subsided. Despite the similarity in their ages and the difference in their backgrounds he felt a paternal concern for his irrepressible young skipper. But there were occasions when he regretted his self-imposed task of protecting Cavendish from the bitter fruits of his own wildness. "I'm sorry, sir. I know the drill," he said after a pause. "Look, Gerry, let's forget rank and Admiralty Instructions and all that guff. I've been a shipmate of yours for almost twelve months now and I know you don't mean any harm with half the things you get up to. But just because some bloody ancestor of yours was one of Nelson's captains at Copenhagen doesn't mean you have to copy him. All right, so it was a good joke in the wardroom when you first suggested the idea. But can't you see that it's sheer bloody lunacy?"

The loudspeaker of the intercom emitted a metallic click as someone flicked the switch in the control room.

"Officer of the Watch to Captain. Shoal water ahead, sir. Will you come to the control room please?"

Cavendish reached for the voice switch to acknowledge the call. Then, picking up his cap, he pulled aside the curtained screen that made up the wardroom's fourth wall. He was his old self again as he paused in the opening.

"Let's keep this little contretemps to ourselves, Nick. I'm not such a lunatic as everyone seems to think. Will you trust me?"

The twinkle in his eyes was irresistible, as many a girl had discovered to her peril, and Hamilton, despite his misgivings, yielded. He got up from the bench and joined Cavendish in the narrow companionway outside the wardroom.

"Okay, but this is definitely the last time. And God help all of us if anything goes wrong."

After the heat of the wardroom Hamilton found the quiet calm of the control room reassuring and comforting. Inside the brightly lit nerve center of the submarine even the monotonous whirring of the deckhead fans and the tingling hum of the motors seemed muted by the silent concentration of the Duty men at their diving stations. And even though most of them suspected that the skipper was up to something, none of their faces showed any trace of anxiety. Their faith in Cavendish was absolute. And, as he looked around the tiny steel vault, Hamilton knew that not a single man would support him if he staged a showdown.

*Surge* was within a mile of Kiel's outer roadstead and Cavendish circled quietly around the compartment as he checked the gauges. He stopped in front of the gyro repeater and then turned to examine the chart. He stepped back satisfied.

"Close up the attack team."

Hamilton wiped the sweat that beaded the palms of his hands on the seat of his trousers. So the stupid bastard was going through with it after all. For a few moments back in the wardroom he had thought that the skipper was going to content himself with surfacing in the middle of the regatta anchorage. That, surely, would have been sensational enough for most men. Even that would be sufficient to spark off a diplomatic incident. Hitler would be only too happy to seize on any opportunity to embarrass his potential enemy. But the quiet order told him that Cavendish intended to see his madcap scheme through to the bitter end. And, as a subordinate officer, he had to carry out the skipper's orders no matter what the consequences.

Cavendish waited while Sub-Lieutenant Sims, the submarine's Fourth Hand, hurried to his attack station in the foreends. He snapped his fingers sharply.

"Up periscope!"

The shoal water was uncomfortably close and for a few seconds Cavendish wondered whether he had stayed in the wardroom a fraction too long. The search lens swung to the left and tilted slightly to locate the port-hand marker buoy rolling gently on the surface to signal the outer margin of the dredged channel.

"Two degrees starboard helm."

"Two degrees starboard, sir. Steering 1-9-5, sir."

"Steady as she goes, Helmsman." Cavendish watched the marker buoy glide past on the port hand. "What depth, Pilot?"

Markham moved to the echo sounder. His place at the chart table had been taken over by the submarine's engineering officer, Lieutenant Kirke, who acted as plotting officer during the attack routine.

"Three fathoms, sir."

Cavendish gave no indication of his private fears as he acknowledged the report with a curt nod. With only eighteen feet of water beneath the keel he knew he was running it close. And he derived no comfort from the knowledge that the dredged channel he had selected was even shallower half a mile ahead. This was the last chance he would have of obtaining accurate data and he wished it had been more reassuring. But the sharp *ping* of the echo-sounder's beam could disclose their presence to the listening ears of the harbor defenses and, ignoring the risk of grounding on an unfriendly German mudbank, he told Markham to switch the apparatus off. From now on he would have to ride the submarine by the seat of his pants.

The search periscope sneaked upwards and Cavendish surveyed the glitter of yachts and warships swinging at anchor in the regatta roadstead. *Gneisenau* lay to starboard and almost beam on. He wondered if Max Müller was on watch. If so he was doubtful of their chances of success. Forewarned was forearmed and Müller was unlikely to lose a £500 wager by default.

"Steer one point to starboard." The bows of the submarine swung slowly to the right in response to the rudder as Cavendish pulled down the microphone link to the fore-ends torpedo flat. "Bring One and Two bow tubes to the ready."

The angle of approach was perfect and, riding snugly at her mooring buoy, the sleek gray battlecruiser was a sitting duck. The strong afternoon sun was behind her bow quarter but, as it was August, it was not sitting low enough in the sky to blind the periscope and *Gneisenau* was clearly silhouetted against the brightness. To the left of her bows lay the two British battleships, *Audacious* and *Arrogant*, guests of honor at the Kiel regatta, and behind them the slim bulk of the battle-cruiser *Leviathan,* Rear Admiral Robertson's flagship—the largest and most famous warship in the world.

For a moment Cavendish wondered what Robertson's reaction would be when the balloon went up. He'd lose his quick Irish temper, that was for sure. But then he'd probably see the funny side of it. Providing, of course, that the Germans didn't open fire and sink the British Squadron then and there. He wondered why he hadn't thought of that possibility before. Perhaps Hamilton was right and he *was* being a bloody lunatic. But the moment of doubt passed quickly and the old madcap demon that prompted most of his actions asserted its dominance again. If he'd calculated correctly everyone would be too flabbergasted to do anything. And by the time they'd recovered from the shock it would be too late. He pushed his face into the rubber cups protecting the eyepieces of the periscope and concentrated on the job in hand.

"Start the attack! Target bearing *that* . . ." Artificer Jackson leaned over the skipper's shoulder to read off the calibrations etched into the brass ring that ran around the circumference of the periscope base.

"182, sir."

Markham set the figure on the dial of the fruit machine—the submarine's torpedo director—and waited for the next piece of data.

"Range *that*!"

Leaning forward again Jackson called off the angle subtended by the difference in inclination of the periscope's top lens in degrees and minutes.

"16 degrees and 12 minutes, sir."

"Down periscope."

Leading Seaman James, back-up link to the torpedo director operator, bent over his slide rule to translate the angle into range. "Range 2,900 yards, sir."

"Two thousand and nine zero zero. Check." Markham fed the distance into his machine, pushed the lever forward, listened to the whirring click of the calculating mechanism, and waited.

Hamilton, standing at his attack station in front of the main blowing and venting panel, also waited. His task was to ensure that *Surge* maintained a constant

15

depth and trim during the final approach but, provided his two coxswains were efficient, there was little for him to do. He could only stare blankly at the banks of dials and glowing warning lights and think. Like every other man in the submarine he was totally ignorant of what was happening on the surface. Only the skipper, peering through his periscope, knew the situation, and the crew had to have perfect trust and confidence in his skill.

Unlike the first officers, however, no member of the submarine's crew had any idea what Cavendish was proposing to do. They knew he was engaged in one of his infamous escapades and, for the most part, they were content to see it through, whatever it was. Only a few older members of the crew felt uneasy and when Cavendish gave the order to bring the torpedo tubes to the ready Coxswain Hawkins took his eyes off the depth gauge for an instant and glanced at the skipper. But Cavendish's expression gave nothing away; Hawkins returned to the task of maintaining the submarine's depth. Shutting the doubts from his mind he sucked his teeth philosophically.

"HE* approaching from starboard, sir. Speed approximately ten knots. Sounds like a pinnace or a small launch."

"Stop motors!" Cavendish reacted instantly to the hydrophone operator's report and the hum of the generators faded into stillness. Cocking his head to one side he listened attentively. The pop-pop-pop of a small inboard engine, magnified by the acoustics of the submarine's hull, was clearly audible inside the control room. "Probably a duty picket-boat," he said easily. "I'll let it clear our range to be on the safe side."

The sound gradually died away to port until only the hydrophone operator could detect the faint burbling exhaust beat and the thrum of the propellor through his sensitive mechanical ears.

"HE bearing to port, sir. 500 yards clear. Moving away."

*Hydrophone Effect.

Cavendish moved back to the narrow-stemmed monocular attack periscope. "Group down—slow ahead both motors. Put me on director angle."

It was an unnecessary instruction. With a stationary target lying broadside onto the submarine's bows the amount of aim-off would be zero. But Cavendish, for all his other faults, was a professional and he saw no point in passing up an opportunity of exercising his attack team under combat conditions. Jackson reached up and set the annular scale of the 'scope to the calibration given to him by the navigator.

"Up periscope!"

The attack 'scope slid upwards, poked above the surface without even a whisper of spray, and angled directly at *Gneisenau*'s broad beam. Cavendish tightened his grip on the handles as the graticule sights came on target. Three sounds . . . two . . . *Surge* rose slightly by the bows and rolled to starboard. A strange slushy sound echoed from beneath the keel.

"Blast!"

Cavendish was surprised by the mildness of the expletive. What a time to run onto a sandbank. Someone was sure to spot them now. *Surge* lurched and slid forward like a seal waddling down to the sea.

"Bow angle up two degrees, sir," the second coxswain reported. "No response from the fore planes."

Cavendish waited impatiently. The inclination to blow the tanks was strong, but if he did the submarine would be exposed on the surface and the anticipated cheers would be replaced by jeers and laughter. He held on as *Surge* scraped its way through the mud. He had no intention of losing his bet now that he'd come this far. But he knew that the range was closing dangerously and, if he delayed altering the helm, the submarine's bows would slam right into the battle-cruiser's armored beam. *Surge* lurched again and this time the movement was more violent.

"Bow angle normal, sir. Running level and holding depth."

Hamilton's quietly casual report was all Cavendish had been waiting for. *Surge* had slithered over the sandbank and was running clear again. A quick check

17

on the gyro repeater showed that the grounding had fortunately not diverted the submarine from its carefully computed attack course and he saw the sights come on target.

"Stand by Bow 1 and 2. Prepare to fire . . . fire!"

No one in the boat knew precisely what was happening. But every man was aware that *Surge* had fired two torpedoes at an unknown target in the middle of Kiel habor. Every eye was on the skipper as they waited. Every eye, that is, except those of the first coxswain. He stared fixedly at his depth gauge and sucked his teeth ruminantly.

"Hitler's going to love us for this," he said to no one in particular.

"Torpedoes running, sir."

The hydrophone report from Leading Seaman Hunniball merely served to confirm their worst fears. What the hell had the skipper done this time?

"Down periscope! Stand by to surface." There was no time for further speculations as the men in the control room moved into their surfacing routine. "Surface!"

"Planes hard a-rise! Close main vents. Blow all tanks."

"Hard a'port, helmsman."

"Full port helm, sir."

"Midships helm!"

"Midships, sir."

Even moving at a funereal two knots *Surge* was closing her erstwhile victim too fast and although she was rising to the surface she had to be kept clear.

"Eight points to port, helmsman!"

It couldn't be done on the rudder alone and, even before the helmsman had acknowledged the order, Cavendish took emergency action.

"Stop starboard motor—full ahead port." He watched the gyro repeater swing as the bows circled to the left. "Stop port motor."

"Fifteen feet, sir."

Cavendish moved unhurriedly toward the steel ladder leading up to the lower hatch set in the curved

18

steel vault of the control room's low deckhand. Pulling the clips, he swung the hatch cover upwards and leaned to one side to avoid the sea water that sluiced down through the opening. The salty tang of fresh sea air wafted down into the crowded compartment and, instinctively, every man took a deep breath into his lungs.

"Ten feet, sir."

"Yeoman, follow me to the bridge. And bring your lamp." Cavendish clambered and reached for the clips of the upper hatch. They slid back easily as he pulled the pins clear.

The heavy hatch cover thrust upwards and Cavendish blinked as the bright August sunlight momentarily blinded his eyes. Then, with a quick heave, he hauled himself up through the narrow opening on to the submarine's bridge.

## CHAPTER TWO

The strident squawk of *Gneisenau*'s A-klaxons penetrated to every compartment of the battle-cruiser's vast hull. The punishment fatigue party painting the narrow spaces making up the honey-combed maze of the warship's double bottom heard it and felt a sudden claustrophobic fear of being trapped. High up in the foremast Seaman 1st Class Georg Schultz was scraping paint from the outside of the gunnery control platform and he experienced the same unreasoning fear as he dropped his tools and came down the rope with the speed of a monkey. And in the crowded wardroom the hubbub of conversation faded to puzzled silence as the loudspeakers brayed their harsh commands.

*"Achtung! Achtung! Secure watertight doors. All hands to collision stations."*

Putting down their glasses the flagship's officers bowed curtly to their guests and hurried out of the wardroom to their divisional stations. The British officers left behind with their counterparts from other German warships looked at each other in astonishment.

"Take no notice, Lieutenant Commander," Kirkelstein told his companion reassuringly. "The *Gneisenau* boys are only showing off. They probably arranged to sound off the alarm bells so they could prove to everyone how efficient they are even when they're apparently caught off guard." He turned and took a glass from the tray held by the steward in silent attendance at the rear of the group. "Have another drink—and don't forget to tell them how smart they were when they come back. It'll make 'em look smugger than ever."

"It seems a funny time to stage a practice alarm," Weatherstone commented as he took the glass from *Emden*'s executive officer.

Kirkelstein shrugged. "It's typical. Flagship captains tend to be exhibitionists. Always trying to make an impression." He swayed slightly and grinned. "If you want to see a crack ship in action you should pay *Emden* a visit before you leave Kiel. We can knock spots off these silly bastards. And we don't need a drill alarm to prove it."

Weatherstone nodded diplomatically, sipped his champagne and cocked half an ear to hear what was happening on deck.

Von Hauptmann put the bridge telephone back on its hook and turned to his two guests.

"My apologies for the disturbance, gentlemen," he said blandly. "There has been some stupid mistake by an over-enthusiastic lookout. *Kapitan* Zembler tells me that someone reported two torpedoes coming toward the ship on the starboard side. And unfortunately, reacting to the report without stopping to think, the officer of the watch sounded the alarm."

Even as he was speaking von Hauptmann and his guests heard two heavy thuds echo from the steel hull plating. They sounded like the thump of a carelessly handled launch banging its bows against the battlecruiser's stout side and the sounds were followed, almost immediately, by a confused babble of shouts from the upper deck level. Robertson thought there was something uncomfortably familiar about the sounds and, putting his glass carefully on the wicker table

20

beside his chair, he stood up and walked unhurriedly to the nearest scuttle. He stared out through the opened port for a few moments in contemplative silence. Then the watchful von Hauptmann saw the admiral's hands suddenly clench. Robertson turned away from the scuttle with a face like thunder.

"There has been no mistake," he announced grimly. "One of my submarines has just surfaced. And at this very moment a couple of British practice torpedoes are floating astern." He paused as he searched for a diplomatic way of escaping from the consequences of the submarine's insolent and inexplicable action. "I must congratulate the *Kriegsmarine* on its alertness, *Herr Vizeadmiral*."

Von Hauptmann bowed politely. He seemed singularly undisturbed by the incident. By contrast, *Kapitan* Mikel's hair literally bristled with indignation. Striding to the porthole with the air of a man who will believe nothing until he has seen it with his own eyes, he stared out through the opened scuttle and visibly swelled with anger. His normally sallow face was puce with rage as he turned to face the British admiral.

"This is an outrage, sir. An insult to the German flag." He turned and bowed stiffly to von Hauptmann. "If you will excuse me, *Herr Vizeadmiral,* I must return to *Koenig* and transmit an immediate report to the Reichschancellery and the *Fuehrer*."

"You will do nothing of the sort, *Herr Kapitan,*" von Hauptmann snapped. "It is nothing more serious than a high-spirited joke by a foolish young officer with more guts than brains. I have no wish to see such a trivial matter blown up into a major diplomatic incident. Admiral Robertson and myself are fully capable of settling the matter without reference to higher authority."

"I quite agree," the British commander-in-chief nodded quickly. Like his German opposite number, he had no wish to see an already delicate situation made worse. He had ever intention of dealing with that damn fool Cavendish—for he had no doubts as to the identity of the culprit—himself. "You may rest assured, *Herr Kapitan,*" he continued, "that I will deal with the officer responsible for this outrage with the greatest severity."

There was no mistaking the sneer on Mikel's face. "I have no doubt you will," he retorted icily. "But that will not be sufficient to efface the insult the British Navy has offered to the German Reich and to our *Fuehrer*." He turned to von Hauptmann. "With respect, *Herr Vizeadmiral*, you cannot forbid me to make a report. You forget that I am not under your command. *Koenig* is present at Kiel as guard-ship for the Foreign Ministry and the Reichminister for Propaganda, *Herr* Goebbels. *Grossadmiral* Raeder grunted *Koenig* independent ship status and has placed me under the direction of the Ministers concerned. While, in deference to your rank and seniority, I would normally obey any order you gave me I regret that in this instance I must follow the instructions of our commander-in-chief."

Raising his right arm in a stiff Nazi salute the *kapitan* clicked his heels and departed importantly through the door of the anteroom.

Von Hauptmann watched him go. He said nothing. Walking across to the drink locker he took down a bottle and poured himself a stiff cognac.

"This could be a bad business, Rear-Admiral," he said gravely. "I fully appreciate that no harm was intended. But . . ." he shrugged and left the rest of the sentence unspoken. He picked up the telephone, pushed the green button and spoke to the bridge. Then, replacing the receiver, he turned to Robertson. "*Kapitan* Zembler tells me that the name of the submarine is *Surge*. Do you know who her captain is?"

"Unfortunately, yes. Lieutenant Commander Cavendish. A very headstrong young man, I'm afraid. He has been in trouble before."

Von Hauptmann nodded. "I believe I have heard of him. Did he not play for the Royal Navy polo team in Malta two years ago? My squadron paid a courtesy visit to the island and I recall witnessing our defeat."

"That was Cavendish," Robertson confirmed. "A brilliant polo player. I daresay you will also remember his father—Admiral George Cavendish. He flew his flag with the Fourth Battle-cruiser Squadron at Jutland in *Redoubtable*. She went down with all hands when one of your shells penetrated her magazines."

"It was a sight I will never forget," von Hauptmann said quietly. He paused at the memory and quickly drained his glass as if to wash it from his mind. "I would like to see this young man Cavendish."

"Not before *I've* seen him," Robertson said grimly. "He and I are going to have a very long chat as soon as I return to my flagship."

"What do you propose to do with him?" Von Hauptmann asked.

"I ought to court-martial the young fool," Robertson said angrily. "But it would only lead to publicity and we must keep this thing out of the papers if we can. I shall have to content myself with a verbal reprimand although I will ensure that Their Lordships are discreetly advised of his foolhardiness. I have little doubt that he will be deprived of his command."

"Don't be too hard on him, Admiral," counseled von Hauptmann. "I know he demonstrated a lamentable lack of judgement but I am sure it was no more than youthful high spirits. England won its Empire with men like that. You can ill-afford to lose them in times like this." He put a reassuring hand on the British admiral's shoulder. "It was a brilliant example of submarine handling," he added with a chuckle. "I am quite sure our *Kommodore* Dönitz will be most impressed by it. Your young man Cavendish could certainly teach our *unterseeboot* commanders a trick or two."

Robertson picked up his cap. "Perhaps, *Herr Vizeadmiral*. But right now I intend to teach him a thing or two myself!"

Von Hauptmann reached for the bridge telephone. "Officer of the Watch? Have the admiral's barge brought alongside at once, please." He replaced the handset and escorted Robertson to the door of the anteroom. "I hope I will see you at the Ball tonight, Admiral?"

"Of course." Robertson paused at the open door. "I think we should endeavor to keep everything normal. At least it will help to reduce the rumors that will be flying around. And do your best to hush up this unfortunate affair, *Vizeadmiral*. You have my word that the culprit will be rigorously punished."

Lieutenant Hamilton wedged himself comfortably into the corner of the wardroom settee, sipped his mug of hot cocoa, and picked up a crumpled copy of yesterday's newspaper.

HM Submarine *Surge*, like a dog in disgrace, had been ordered out of the main anchorage by the commander-in-chief and was moored to a rusty buoy in a stagnant backwater out of sight of the city. Out of sight, perhaps, but most certainly not out of smell for the prevaling wind swept the aroma of Kiel's gas works' through the opened hatches where it mingled fetidly with the sour smell wafting across the black waters from the local sewage outfall. As he tried to concentrate on the trivia of the *Daily Mirror* Hamilton had time to reflect on the events of the day subsequent to the mock attack on *Gneisenau*.

A peremptory signal from the flagship had summoned Cavendish to the august presence of the commander-in-chief at 1600 hours and he had departed shortly afterwards, nonchalant as ever and outwardly unconcerned by the furore he had caused. Thirty minutes later a further signal had ordered the submarine to weigh anchor and proceed to her new berth in Aaschlandt Creek. Hamilton had received his own orders to report to the flagship just before 1800 hours and the added injunction to bring the submarine's log with him boded ill for someone.

"There's a hell of a bloody row going on," the midshipman in charge of the picket boat told him as he stepped down from the submarine's rusty foredeck casing into the spotlessly scrubbed well deck.

"What has happened to Lieutenant Commander Cavendish?" Hamilton was stiffly formal. As a full-ranking lieutenant he had no intention of gossiping with a mere wart.*

"Old Bobs has put him under arrest—or that's what I heard in the gunroom before I left," the midshipman said casually. "Old Bobs" was Rear Admiral Robertson's nickname. Despite his fiery Irish temper he was held in high esteem by both officers and men and his bark was notoriously worse than his bite. "They apparently had a hell of a row."

"You shouldn't listen to rumors." Hamilton admonished him coldly, conveniently overlooking the fact that he had asked the question. Taking his place in the sternsheets he remained there in dignified silence for the rest of the trip. The picket boat weaved and twisted through the lines of moored yachts and anchored warships. The coxswain swung the boat in a wide arc as he approached the battle-cruiser. Cut the engine switches, the launch lost speed at precisely the right moment, passed under *Leviathan*'s stern and came alongside the starboard gangway. Jackson, the able seaman in the bows, lowered his boathook from the "present" position above his head and skilfully caught the looped line dangling beneath the bottom platform of the gangway.

Hamilton came up the sternsheets, acknowledged the salutes of the midshipman and coxswain, and stepped onto the landing platform as the picket-boat's rubbing strake grazed the companionway.

The officer of the watch was waiting to greet him as he came up the ladder and, having punctiliously saluted the quarter-deck in accordance with ancient custom, Hamilton introduced himself with admirable brevity.

"Lieutenant Hamilton. First Officer HM Submarine *Surge*."

De Courcy returned the salute with a friendly grin. "Welcome aboard. I hope you'll get an easier passage than your skipper. 'Bobs' is leaping up and down like a leprechaun dancing a jig on a red-hot boiler." He turned to the duty midshipman waiting discreetly in the rear. "Wake up, Bonzo! Take Lieutenant Hamilton to

*Royal Navy slang for a midshipman.

25

the admiral's quarters. And for heaven's sake don't do anything that'll make the old man's temper any worse."

"Of course my name's not really Bonzo," the midshipman told Hamilton with adolescent seriousness as he led the lieutenant in the direction of the admiral's cloistered suite in the stern. "Old Courty calls all his doggies* that. One of these days I'm sure he'll pat me on the head and give me a biscuit."

Hamilton smiled. Like all commissioned officers he'd gone through the same petty humiliations when he'd been a snotty. "It could be worse," he said encouragingly. "The commander of *Essex* used to call me Fido when I was on the China station. You'll get used to it," he chuckled. "And you never know—it might be a chocolate biscuit." He followed the midshipman down a short companionway leading to the pristine whiteness and burnished brass of the quarter-deck. "Who was that bumptious little toad in charge of the duty picket boat?"

"You must mean Oliver—God's gift to the Royal Navy. Well, *he* thinks he is, anyway. Don't you like him either, sir?"

"Not much. I'm glad to see you don't stoop to gossip."

Bonzo grinned cheekily. He wasn't used to Hamilton's brand of instant comradeship. Most of the lieutenants he encountered on the big ships were officious stiff-necked martinets. Perhaps, he decided suddenly, he'd volunteer for the Trade* when he'd passed out of his sub-lieutenant's course at Greenwich next year. If Hamilton was any guide, submarine officers seemed to be good sorts. And a bloody sight more human than the two-ringers who lorded it around the flagship.

"I daresay I would if I could, sir," he admitted. "But no one tells a wart much. Oliver only pretends he knows something because his elder brother's in our wardroom. He puts it on a bit."

---

*Naval slang for the midshipman attached to the commander and often used for any midshipman assisting a ranking officer.
*Royal Navy parlance for the submarine service.

Bonzo stopped outside a heavy, armored door. The marine sentry guarding the entrance snapped smartly to attention and presented arms with his well-oiled and polished Lee-Enfield. Hamilton saluted and nodded the midshipman to enter the holy of holies. The expression on Bonzo's face was that of a sinner about to go into a forbidden temple.

The white-painted passage behind the armor was pleasantly cool and the lieutenant could feel the soft chill of the air-conditioning fans on his skin. Bonzo glanced at his companion nervously, straightened his tie, and swallowed hard as if preparing for his ultimate doom. Then, taking his courage in both hands, he rapped sharply on the stout oak door of the admiral's day cabin.

"Come!"

Bonzo opened the door timidly, stepped nervously over the threshold, and twitched to a salute.

"Yes, boy?" All warts were "boy" to Robertson.

"Please, sir. Lieutenant Hamilton, sir."

"Well send him in, boy."

Bonzo blanched, saluted again, and scurried out. Rear Admiral Robertson waited until the door was firmly closed. Then he turned his attention to his next victim.

"Speak up, Mr. Hamilton. What do you have to say for yourself?"

"Nothing, sir."

The cold blue eyes appraised him shrewdly. "Surely you knew what that young fool Cavendish was planning to do?" Robertson barked.

Hamilton nodded. "I thought he was joking, sir. It was only when we got inside Kiel Bay and he ordered the Attack Team to close up that I realized he was serious. It was too late to do anything by that time."

"Is that all you can say in your defense, Lieutenant?"

"Yes, sir. I was under orders. I do not see that I can be held responsible for my commanding officer's actions."

Robertson's belligerent stare softened. "I'm sorry, my boy. I didn't mean to accuse you of anything." His squared shoulders drooped slightly and he rubbed his chin. "It's a bad business," he said quietly and Hamilton felt a sudden sympathy for the commander-in-chief. "The Germans have taken it very well, all things considered. But I suspect that there could still be trouble somewhere along the line. One or two members of the German government have been looking for an excuse like this. Heaven knows what might happen if they get their way." Robertson paced slowly up and down the day cabin like a fretful lion. He stopped suddenly and glared at Hamilton. "Why the devil didn't you stop the idiot?" he demanded.

"I made a formal protest, sir. But Cavendish insisted I did it by the book. I was told to obey orders and lodge a complaint afterwards."

"And do you propose to lodge such a complaint, Lieutenant?"

Hamilton hesitated. It was the one question he had dreaded Robertson asking. "I don't know, sir," he said simply. "I'd like to give it more thought."

"The time for thinking is over, Mr. Hamilton!" the rear admiral snapped sharply. "I want a decision. Do you intend to make a formal complaint in writing against Lieutenant Commander Cavendish? I cannot decide my own course of action until I know."

A knock on the cabin door gave Hamilton a momentary reprieve to gather his thoughts. Robertson looked up at the interruption.

"Come!"

The door opened and Commander Drury, the Fleet wireless officer, entered the cabin clutching a pink signal flimsy in his hand. He looked hot and bothered and he glanced questioningly at Hamilton. The rear admiral waved his hand impatiently.

"Priority signal from the admiralty, sir," Drury said quickly. "When I saw the prefix I decoded it personally." He handed it to the admiral and waited. Robertson pulled a pair of glasses from his top pocket, thrust them on his nose, and studied the signal intently. Then, having read it through again, he put the flimsy down on top of his desk for his secretary, Paymaster Commander Lerwick, to docket and file. He looked up at Drury as he removed his glasses.

"Thank you, Commander. Will you send an immediate reply to the first lord." He waited while Drury produced a pencil and notepad. "From C-in-C, Special Duty Squadron, Kiel, to Naval Secretary, First Lord. Your 16–54 refers. Recommend . . . no, make that, strongly recommend . . . no hasty action. Full report follows. Officer concerned removed from his command. Robertson. Have you got that, Drury?" He waited while the FWO read it back. He nodded. "Good—now get that transmitted to cypher immediately. And keep me informed of all messages relating to this incident."

"Very good, sir."

"And one other thing. Will you keep a couple of your telegraphists on duty to monitor all radio broadcasts from London and Berlin. I want a transcript of all news bulletins."

The commander saluted and went out, wondering where the hell he was going to find a telegraphist who could understand and translate German radio bulletins. He decided he'd probably have to do it himself.

"Well, that settles it," Robertson said with a shrug of finality. "It's a court-martial affair now." Hamilton said nothing. Despite his curiosity about the signal Drury had brought in he knew it was not his place to ask what it contained. But it sounded black for Cavendish whatever it was. "The Foreign Office has received a Note from von Ribbentrop,"* the rear admiral continued. Despite Hamilton's relatively junior rank he seemed glad to have someone to talk to. "They want the culprit's head on a platter, I gather. Whitehall's in a hell of a flap. The Commander-in-Chief Portsmouth has been ordered to prepare a court-martial immediately the squadron returns to England."

Robertson walked across the opened port on the starboard side of the cabin and stared out over the lines of yachts and flag-bedecked warships.

"You may return to your ship, Lieutenant," he said, bringing the interview to a close without turning his

*Hitler's Minister for Foreign Affairs.

head away from the scuttle. "I want you to take over temporary command until Captain Middleton arrives this evening. Leave the log-book on my desk as you go out."

Hamilton put the book down as directed and saluted the rear admiral's unseeing back. Then, closing the door behind him, he made his way down the narrow white-painted passage and stepped out on deck. The air smelled fresh and sweet after the oppressive tension in the admiral's quarters and he took a deep breath.

Why the devil was Middleton, a full-ranking post captain and senior officer of the two Rosyth submarine flotillas, coming over to Kiel, Hamilton wondered as he retraced his footsteps toward the quarterdeck companionway. He shrugged. Middleton presumably wanted to ferret out a few facts before the court-martial was convened. As the officer responsible for Cavendish's appointment in command of *Surge,* Middleton was probably worried about the effect of the incident on his own career. Competition for promotion to flag-rank was fierce and even the slightest criticism could damn his chances forever.

Hamilton knew that Middleton wasn't coming over just to take *Surge* back. As a fully qualified watch-keeping officer he was quite capable of commanding the submarine without supervision. There had to be another reason. Perhaps Middleton was coming over to keep an eye on *him.* Hamilton stopped suddenly beside one of the battle-cruiser's 4.7″ AA guns as the thought struck him for the first time. As the submarine's executive officer it was well on the cards that he might find himself standing alongside Cavendish as one of the accused when the court-martial finally took place. It was a factor he hadn't considered before. And with Cavendish's connections in high places there was always the chance that a large portion of the responsibility would be passed onto his own shoulders. Perhaps that was why Robertson had asked him why he hadn't done anything to stop his commanding officer.

De Courcy was still pacing the deck in front of the gangway. He looked up with his usual cheerful grin as he saw Hamilton approaching.

"What's happening?"

Hamilton shrugged. Discretion seemed the better part of valor and he decided to say nothing of the first lord's signal. It was a delicate situation and the fewer people who knew, the better it would be for everyone. Cavendish was a popular officer and if the lower deck got to hear of the court-martial while they were still guests of the German Navy they were likely to cause a riot when they went ashore.

"Usual flap," he said vaguely. "You know what the top brass are like—lots of noises but they never tell you anything."

De Courcy nodded sympathetically. "I know what you mean. I was in the Med when the *Royal Oak* mutiny blew up. We had to wait for the London newspapers to arrive before we found out what was going on in our own squadron." He grinned. "I wouldn't worry about it too much. Gerry Cavendish will wriggle out of it somehow. He always does."

That's precisely what I'm afraid of, thought Hamilton. But he kept his thoughts to himself and nodded his agreement.

"I daresay you're right," he said with a shrug. "Can you call up my boat? I've got to get back to *Surge*— Bobs has given me temporary command!"

De Courcy passed an instruction to the duty petty officer and Hamilton heard the veteran's bull-like roar as he called the picket-boat alongside the companionway to pick up its passenger.

"I suppose I ought to have piped you over the side now that you're skipper of your own ship," de Courcy grinned mischievously.

"Don't bother," Hamilton said shortly. "I doubt if I'll be in command very long. They seem to be sharpening their knives in Whitehall already."

"Bad as that?"

Hamilton wondered if he had said too much. He shrugged and walked to the upper stage of the gangway. "Not really," he said with a forced laugh. "Probably only my guilty conscience pricking me over past sins."

Midshipman Oliver saluted as the lieutenant stepped

down into the battle-cruiser's steam pinnace. He made no effort to conceal his annoyance at being kept waiting. The harbor tender was due to leave with the official guests for the Regatta Ball in less than an hour and here he was still on duty in his working rig playing chauffeur to a bloody two-ringer. That was the trouble with wardroom officers, they didn't give a damn for the gun-room.

In normal circumstances Hamilton would have rounded on the wart for insolence and given him the length of his not inconsiderable tongue. But, for the moment, he had more important things to worry about than disciplining junior officers. Ignoring the black looks he took his place in the sternsheets and ordered Oliver to take him back to the insalubrious mudbanks of Aaschlandt Creek where *Surge* was doing penance for her sins.

And now, with the excitements of the day thankfully behind him, Hamilton relaxed in the submarine's tiny wardroom sipping hot cocoa from the galley while he pondered on what the immediate future held in store for him. In retrospect his interview with Rear Admiral Robertson had hardly been reassuring. And it was not difficult to see which way the wind was blowing. But any further thoughts were interrupted as Markham, *Surge*'s navigation officer, pulled the wardroom curtains aside and squeezed into the little cubby hole that served as their communal mess.

"What do they intend to do with the skipper?" he asked cheerfully. "Hang him from the nearest yardarm?"

"Not quite," Hamilton said. "But I gather there are one or two people at the admiralty who'd like to, given half the chance."

Markham helped himself to cocoa and settled comfortably into the wardroom's solitary armchair. He was eight years younger than Hamilton but, as a cadet entrant from Dartmouth, he was only eighteen months junior to the first officer on the seniority list. He wasn't too sure about commissioning officers from the lower deck but he was fair-minded enough to admit that

Hamilton was a good seaman, and a good deal more level-headed than most of his contemporaries.

"We had a signal from *Leviathan* just before you got back, Nick. It's a pity it's not in happier circumstances but congratulations on being appointed in command." He lit a cigarette and blew a plume of smoke from his nose. "We'll all miss the Old Man, of course, but you can count on us to back you up."

"Thanks, John." Hamilton filled his pipe slowly. "Tell me something—did you know about Gerry's plan to fire practice torpedos at the German Fleet?"

"No. He hadn't said a word to me about it. I could tell by your face that something was up and my plot showed me we were heading into Kiel Bay when he told the Attack Team to close up. Even then I merely assumed he'd been authorized to carry out some sort of demonstration torpedo exercise at a prearranged target."

"Would you have stopped him had you known what he intended to do?"

Markham drew on his cigarette as he considered Hamilton's question. "I honestly don't know," he said after a long pause. "But knowing Gerry I think I'd have kept my mouth shut. The skipper wasn't the sort of man you could argue with once he'd given his orders."

"I know. He threw the book at me when I tried." Hamilton put the pipe in his mouth, tamped down the tobacco, and held a match over the bowl. He waited until it was glowing red. "Did *anyone* know what he was up to?"

"I don't think so. Mind you, I'm sure a couple of the older hands guessed what he was proposing to do when we started the final attack run. But no one asks questions when a submarine's closed up for action."

"Do you think anyone would have supported me if I'd faced him out in the control room?"

Markham shook his head. "Not a chance, Nick. Our ship's company are the wildest bunch of pirates in the Trade. They'd have backed Gerry to the hilt no matter what he did. You know he's like a god to them."

"And you too?"

33

The navigator stubbed his cigarette out in the tin lid that served as the wardroom's ashtray. He looked up sharply. "What's the cross-examination for, Nick? What's done is done. There's no point in having a *post mortem* about it."

"Well that's exactly what Whitehall intends to do," Hamilton said. "Robertson had a signal from the first lord while I was with him. Gerry is going to be court-martialed." He sucked on his pipe. "And as I seem to be the only one who knew about the plan in advance I reckon I'm for the high jump as well."

Markham made no comment but the expression on his face reflected his unspoken agreement with Hamilton's pessimistic prediction.

"I'm sure Robertson wanted to hush the whole thing up," Hamilton went on. "But apparently Gerry's Nazi friends don't have a sense of humor. Von Ribbentrop put a formal complaint to London and, in an effort to keep the peace, the Foreign Office have demanded a court-martial."

Markham lit another cigarette. "It doesn't say much for Gerry's Nazi pals. I thought they had plenty of influence."

"More likely they've been using him." Hamilton knocked his pipe out into the tin lid. "He mentioned something about having a wager with an officer on *Gneisenau*. I reckon someone put him up to the whole thing, knowing full well it would create a diplomatic incident. It's a typical Nazi trick if you ask me." He slipped the pipe into his pocket, drained the last dregs of cocoa from his mug, and stood up with a yawn. "I've had enough for one day. I'm for my bunk."

Markham yawned in sympathy.

"Me too. I'm down for the morning watch."

Hamilton took off his jacket and began to unbutton his shirt. Hanging his clothes up neatly, he slipped into his pyjamas and climbed into his bunk. He had decided against moving into Cavendish's cabin for the moment. Sailors were unduly sensitive to small things and the skipper had been a popular officer. If they thought he was stepping into Cavendish's shoes too eagerly it could cause resentment and Hamilton was already all too aware that the atmosphere inside the submarine would soar to boiling point once the ship's company learned of the court-martial.

"I'll check the watch bill in the morning," he told Markham as he settled back on the pillow. "We'll be one short until we get a replacement so we may need to double up duties."

"Very good, sir." Markham had adapted himself to their new relationship without difficulty. "I'll get the fourth hand to bring you the watch bill after breakfast." He pulled himself up onto the top bunk and banged down the pillow.

"Good night, sir."

"Good night, John, and thanks."

*Captain to the bridge!*

Hamilton loked up from the official papers scattered over the narrow kneehole desk squeezed into one corner of the captain's tiny cabin as the metallic voice crackled through the intercom loudspeaker grill. He was about to ignore the request and continue writing out the new watch bill when he realized with a start that the call was for his own presence on the bridge. It was difficult to adjust to the fact that he, and not Gerry Cavendish, was now the commanding officer of *HMS Surge*.

Picking up his cap and pushing aside the curtains, he made his way along the communications passage to the control room. Chief Petty Officer Hawkins, the submarine's coxswain, was busy checking the forward hydroplane controls for signs of damage as a result of their brief grounding the previous day, and he straightened to attention as Hamilton ducked through the opening in the watertight bulkhead.

"Morning, sir."

Hamilton returned the salute.

"Good morning, Cox'n. What's all the panic on deck?"

"Dunno, sir. I thought I heard the pilot say there was a boat coming alongside." He managed to convey the impression that, whatever it was, it was nothing to do with *him*.

35

"You'd better get cleaned up, Cox'n. Might be a VIP coming to visit us and we want to show 'em we're still a taut ship."

Hamilton swung himself onto the steel ladder and climbed up through the lower compartment of the conning-tower. Markham was waiting as he hauled himself up through the shoulder-wide hatch onto the submarine's bridge.

"*Leviathan*'s picket boat coming alongside, sir," he reported. "I can't quite see who's in it but it seems to be a post captain."

"It's probably Middleton," Hamilton told him. "Robertson said he was flying over. You'd best get down to receive him aboard. And tell Brightman to pipe him over the side."

The picket boat bumped gently against the weed-fringed ballast tanks and its bow number grabbed the line thrown down by *Surge*'s deck party. He held the launch steady while Captain Middleton stepped up onto the submarine's forecasing. Markham tucked the telescope under his left arm, came to attention, and saluted as the bos'n's pipe shrilled its traditional greeting. Then, after a few brief words of welcome, he escorted Middleton to the bridge to meet Hamilton.

"Good morning, sir. Nice to have you aboard."

"I've no time for all that, Lieutenant," Middleton snapped testily. "I want to talk to you in the wardroom. And make sure we are not disturbed."

Hamilton nodded to Markham and, as he led Middleton down the conning-tower ladder, he heard the navigator passing the necessary instructions down the voicepipe. By the time they reached the curtained entrance to the wardroom Coxswain Hawkins, smart and tidy in his Number Ones, was already standing guard. How he had washed, shaved, and changed in such a short period was a mystery but Hamilton had long since given up wondering how senior petty officers consistently achieved the impossible when occasion demanded. Hawkins saluted the officers and looked curiously at Middleton. He wondered what he wanted with Hamilton. The top brass were certainly in a hell of a flap over something and Hawkins wasn't sorry he was well out of it. Yet, with the typical contrariness of a true veteran, he resented the fact that he was being kept in the dark.

The two men vanished behind the curtained privacy of the wardroom. And, standing guard at the bulkhead door, Hawkins cocked his ear like a terrier listening for a rabbit in the long grass. He was, however, doomed to disappointment. The heavy drapes deadened the sound of the voices into an inaudible mumble and his curiosity had to remain unsatisfied.

Middleton wasted no time on polite preliminaries. He had come to Kiel with a specific job and he intended to do it.

"I assume you are aware of the reason for my visit?" he asked Hamilton curtly. The lieutenant nodded. "Very well," he continued, "in that case you will not be unduly surprised by the next question. Do you still intend to make a Paragraph 8 complaint against Lieutenant Commander Cavendish?"

Hamilton had already spent a sleepless night considering the matter.

"Yes, sir," he said firmly.

He had no wish to cut Gerry's throat—the silly bastard was in more than enough trouble already. But he had his own career to think of and his prior knowledge of Cavendish's plan to "Copenhagen" the German fleet placed him in an awkward position. If he withdrew the complaint at this stage his action could be construed to mean that he was giving his tacit approval to the escapade. And he could easily find himself facing court-martial charges as well.

Captain Middleton made it obvious that he did not approve of Hamilton's answer. He frowned darkly and puffed his neck like a cobra preparing to strike.

"I think you are being a trifle unwise in the circumstances, Lieutenant." The abrasive rasp in his voice softened as he planted the carefully prepared seed of doubt. "If it is proved—and I have no doubt it will be—that your commanding officer was engaged on an exercise designed to provide information of the greatest assistance to the admiralty, a complaint on your part will only succeed in bringing your own judgement into question." Middleton paused for a moment. "You are an ambitious officer, are you not, Lieutenant?"

"Yes, sir."

"Then I suggest you think deeply on what I have said before you rush off and lodge this complaint. Competition for the 'perisher'* is keen. An error of judgement like this could easily lose you a place on the course."

Hamilton disliked blackmail and Middleton's bull-dozing tactics only served to reinforce his determination to stick to his guns. But he was uncomfortably aware of the fact that, as Markham had warned him earlier, no one else on the submarine was likely to back him up."

"My complaint is already drafted, sir," he said stiffly. "I would, however, like to see the log to verify certain facts before I finalize it."

"The ship's log has been impounded as evidence, Lieutenant. Neither you nor anyone else will be able to see it until it is produced to the court." Middleton paused for a moment before changing the direction of his attack. "How many German destroyers did *Surge* evade during the run up to Kiel?"

"I have no idea, sir. Lieutenant Commander Cavendish was the only person to take observations through the periscope and he gave no indication of what was happening on the surface."

"But there *were* various course changes?"

"Yes, sir," Hamilton agreed.

"And on two occasions he ordered the motors to be stopped?"

"That is correct, sir."

The corners of Middleton's mouth curled smugly in a complacent smile. "I am pleased to hear you confirm what Cavendish told me last night," he said enigmatically. "I will say no more—the matter is *sub judice* in any case—but I recommend you to consider my questions carefully. There is a great deal more in this affair than meets the eye."

* Naval slang for the commanding officer's course at the Periscope School.

"I'm sure there is, sir," Hamilton conceded. And I wonder how *you* fit into the jig-saw, he asked himself. "Will that be all, sir?"

"Yes, that's all, Lieutenant. I must get back to the flagship. I think I have covered all the points I had in mind." He knew Hamilton was an ambitious young man and coming up from the ranks made him a late starter in the promotion stakes. He paused for a moment and then dangled the carrot temptingly as a parting shot in the battle. "Robertson wanted me to take *Surge* back to Rosyth but I told him you were more than capable of handling her. By the way, there's another 'perisher' starting in October. A couple more feathers in your cap like this and I'm sure you'll be on it." He returned Hamilton's salute and pulled the curtain aside. "Don't bother to see me over the side, Lieutenant. I'm sure you have more than enough to do without fussing over uninvited guests. The officer of the day can do me the necessary honors."

Hamilton found his pipe and started to fill it as Middleton went through the curtain. He heard Hawkins stamp to attention and then the echoing clatter of leather soles on the steel deck plating faded toward the control room. Standing motionless in the middle of the wardroom with his pipe poised halfway to his mouth he thought back over the strange interview.

*Two* feathers in his cap? Well, one of them would obviously be bringing *Surge* safely back to Rosyth under his temporary command. But two . . . ? It was clear from what Middleton had said that his complaint against Cavendish was expected to form the cornerstone of the prosecution's case at the court-martial. So the second feather would be his reward for getting his former skipper off the hook. Hamilton lit his pipe and stared thoughtfully at his carefully drafted report to Rear Admiral Robertson.

# CHAPTER THREE

"With the court's permission I would like to recall an earlier witness—Lieutenant Nicholas Hamilton, the first officer of *HMS Surge*."

Captain Davidge-Pitts, president of the court, signified his approval with an almost imperceptible nod and, as the master-at-arms hurried out to fetch the witness, he leaned forward and whispered something to the deputy judge advocate.

It was the second day of the trial and despite the efforts of the electric fans, the atmosphere inside the makeshift courtroom was turgid and stuffy. The ports were wide open and unscreened but the armored deck overhead seemed to absorb the fierce heat of the August sun until the steel bulkheads glowed like the walls of a baking oven. The temperature inside the hangar deck of *HMS Argonaut,* hastily cleared of aircraft and converted into a courtroom with the aid of asbestos fire curtains, stood at a fraction over 90° but, despite the oppressive heat, Davidge-Pitts, a stickler for rules and regulations, had not granted permission for jackets to be removed.

Hamilton entered the court, saluted the president, and took his place on the witness stand for a second time. He had given his evidence-in-chief the previous afternoon. The defense had handled him with courteous politeness on his first appearance and his cross-examination had been cursory and brief. But it was clear that Sir Abel Bullivant, in his capacity as friend of the accused, had not wished to play his hand too early in the proceedings and he had been content to probe one or two minor details in Hamilton's evidence and no more.

Davidge-Pitts put down his papers and looked across as the new witness took his place on the stand.

"I must remind you, Lieutenant, that this is a continuation of the evidence you gave the court yesterday and that you are still under oath."

40

"I understand, sir."

The president glanced at the accused's friend. "You may carry on, Sir Abel."

Sir Abel Bullivant KC was a formidable figure. His face was obscenely fat with heavy jowls and a large hooked nose that curved over a pair of thick lips. His wig and gown looked incongruous against the grim gray background of the aircraft-carrier's steel-decked hangar and the blue uniforms, gleaming buttons, and gold lace of the court-martial board. As he walked slowly toward the witness stand he resembled a large black bird trailing its wings as it stalked its prey.

He was costing Cavendish 500 guineas a day, but he was worth every penny of his fee as many an acquitted prisoner in the Central Criminal Court could testify. And there was little doubt that the card he had played in his opening speech for the defense together with the contents of Cavendish's statement had made a considerable impression upon the court. Now it only remained for him to destroy the prosecution's main witness and the case was won.

He consulted his notes carefully, timing the delay in his first question with the skill of a Spanish inquisitor to heighten the nervousness of his victim; then looked up with a sudden jerk of his head—one of the idiosyncracies that had become a trademark of his forensic technique.

"You testified earlier that when you first heard of the plan from the accused you regarded it as no more than a joke."

"That is correct."

"When did you realize that it was not, in fact, a joke but a carefully prepared scheme?"

Hamilton wondered where the questions were leading. As a witness, he had not been in court to hear Sir Abel's opening speech outlining the case for the defense. "When I heard the accused order the torpedo crew to close up soon after we had entered Kiel Fjord."

"Very well—so it was no longer a joke. It was something else. What was your reaction?"

"I thought he was raving mad."

Bullivant smiled to himself as if sharing a private joke with the witness. "I see. So, in your own words, you thought he was raving mad." He paused for a moment. "This was presumably the moment when you asked to speak to the accused and had this argument about illegal orders."

"More or less, sir. I only requested permission to speak to him in the control room. The discussion about the legality of the orders took place in the wardroom where no one else could overhear us."

"Tell me, Lieutenant," Bullivant's voice was almost purring. "Why did you agree to carry out the orders but subsequently make a formal complaint against those self-same orders to the commander-in-chief?"

"It is the procedure laid down in King's Regulations and Admiralty Instructions, sir."

Bullivant looked up sharply. The purr had become a whiplash. "But you have just told the court you thought your commanding officer was raving mad."

Captain Dalby, the prosecutor, rose swiftly to his feet and stopped Bullivant before he could continue further.

"I object. The witness is not an expert and has not been called as such. He canot express an opinion on the sanity or otherwise of the accused."

Davidge-Pitts nodded his head in agreement. "I must uphold the prosecutor's objection, Sir Abel."

Bullivant bowed indulgently. "With the court's permission I will rephrase the question." He turned back to the bewildered Hamilton. "Are you aware, Lieutenant, that precedents exist where a junior officer can arrest his superior in certain circumstances?"

Hamilton shook his head. "No, sir. I was not aware of such procedures."

Captain Dalby was on his feet again. He had already spotted the direction of Bullivant's cross-examination and he had to somehow maintain the credibility of the prosecution's key witness.

"If the accused's friend is referring to the case of *HMS Torch* in 1872 I must remind him that, in that instance, the commanding officer was drunk—not mad. I would submit that it is easier for a layman to conclude that someone is drunk than to decide he is mad—especially when the senior officer concerned is one's own captain."

Davidge-Pitts looked around the court sternly as a ripple of laughter spread through the room but he could not repress the twinkle in his own eyes as he replied:

"I would think there are many occasions when a junior officer concludes that his captain is mad. I must plead guilty to the offense myself." He turned to Hamilton. "What did you mean by the word, Lieutenant?"

"I did not intend to imply that the accused was insane, sir. I was using the word loosely—meaning that he was being foolish."

Davidge-Pitts nodded and looked across at Bullivant. "Scarcely adequate grounds for Lieutenant Hamilton to arrest his commanding officer I think you will agree, Sir Abel."

Bullivant's jowls reddened as he stood up. He was not used to being worsted in court. He had clearly underestimated Captain Dalby and he resolved not to make the same mistake again. He bowed to the president.

"I will not pursue the matter further, sir. I am obliged to you for clarifying the witness's misuse of the English language." Bullivant was glad that he had been able to salvage something on which he could spit his venom. "With the court's permission I will turn to the facts of the defense's case, namely, that the so-called attack was part of a carefully laid plan to discover the efficiency of the German Navy's anti-submarine detection equipment." He turned his attention back to Hamilton. "Captain Middleton has testified that, during a discussion with you on the day after the incident, you agreed that *Surge* had altered course on several occasions during the attack run and had also stopped motors. Is this correct—or were you misusing the English language again?"

Hamilton ignored the barb. So that was why Middleton had asked him those apparently innocent questions when he'd visited the submarine that day. But

43

how the hell did Gerry have the nerve to put this crazy story forward about testing German anti-submarine devices? He took a deep breath.

"Captain Middleton's testimony is correct, sir," he agreed quietly.

Bullivant nodded. "I would just like to ensure there is no misunderstanding on this point, Lieutenant. The hearing is *in camera* so you may speak quite freely. Lieutenant Commander Cavendish carried out the dummy attack in combat conditions in order to discover whether the German Navy had perfected detection devices similar to our Asdic apparatus. Did he give any indication of this to you at the time?"

"No, sir," Hamilton said truthfully.

"Well there is no harm in that, I think. It would be natural for him to keep such a plan to himself." Bullivant turned to the deputy judge advocate. "Will you please produce the log of *HMS Surge*—Exhibit No 2, I believe." He glanced at Captain Davidge-Pitts. "The log is, of course, already sworn in evidence."

The president nodded his agreement and Bullivant returned to the witness. "You told Captain Middleton that the accused had changed course on several occasions. How long after passing Buelk Point was the first helm direction given?"

"It is difficult to say, sir . . . probably about five minutes."

Bullivant took the logbook from the deputy judge advocate and ran his finger down the entries. "Let me see . . . *14-03. Buelk Point directly abeam. Submerged. Depth 30 feet.*" The friend of the accused paused and then passed to the next entry. *"14-09. Half speed. Course 1-9-0."* He looked up at Hamilton. "That appears to confirm your estimate, Lieutenant. Do you know the reason for the course and speed alteration?"

"Lieutenant Commander Cavendish reduced speed to conserve the batteries. I believe he altered course because he wished to keep to the middle of the deep channel."

"A prudent decision on both counts?"

"Yes, sir."

Bullivant glanced down at the opened logbook. "And when was the next alteration in course?" he asked.

"I really could not say, sir. I was not keeping the log and I was busy controlling the trim."

"You would oblige me by trying, Lieutenant."

Hamilton felt sure the barrister was leading him into a trap and he looked across at Davidge-Pitts for guidance before answering.

"This is an important part of the evidence," the president told him. "You are, of course, not obliged to say anything that might incriminate you but I am instructed by my superiors that no action will be taken against you should you do so. They regard this matter as one of vital national importance and only seek to establish the truth."

Hamilton felt the weight lift from his shoulders. So they didn't intend to shift the responsibility onto him. But in that case what the devil was Bullivant up to? He bowed his thanks to the board.

"Thank you, sir. To the best of my recollection there were a series of course changes about twenty minutes later—after Lieutenant Commander Cavendish and myself had returned to the control room."

"That would be about . . . 14-30." Bullivant looked down at the log. "Ah, yes, here we are: *14-31. Altered course to pass close to destoyer* Hans Ludemann. *Passed at distance of 200 yards. No detection observed.*" Sir Abel paused and looked up at the witness. "Were you aware of the reason for the alteration in course?"

"No, sir. Only the officer at the periscope is aware of the surface situation. And that was, of course, the accused."

"There was no reason why he should tell you about the destroyer?"

"No, although it is usual practice for the captain to report back on what he can see through the periscope."

Bullivant ignored Hamilton's supplementary explanation. He was in sight of his target and was closing in for the kill. "You were running at what I believe is known as silent speed?"

"That is correct."

"A speed which would be barely perceptible on normal hydrophones?"

"Subject to range—yes, sir."

Bullivant positively beamed. "So it would be reasonable to conclude that if a number of destroyers or anti-submarine vessels were evaded by *HMS Surge,* and assuming that the submarine passed reasonably close to them, the German Navy does not possess detection devices similar to our Asdic sets?"

"Yes, sir. I think that would be a reasonable conclusion to draw."

"Do you recall any other course changes, Lieutenant?"

"Only vaguely, sir."

"But there *were* other changes?"

"Yes."

Bullivant studied the log book again. "Will the court permit me to read two further entries? *14-43. Sighted destroyer of Maas class moving on a northerly course at approximately ten knots. Passed across bows at range of 300 yards. Not detected.* And again . . . *14-49. Passed within 100 yards of destroyer* Ernst Heinemann. *Not detected.*" Bullivant snapped the logbook shut. "It would seem that your evidence supports the logbook entries."

Sir Abel paused to allow Hamilton time to deny his statement and, when he remained silent, he handed the logbook back to the deputy judge advocate.

"There is just one other point to clear up, Lieutenant. I believe that, on *HMS Surge* and contrary to King's Regulations, the log was kept by the captain and not by the navigator."

Hamilton hesitated and then nodded. "That is correct, sir."

"Although, on occasions, for example when the submarine dived at 14-03, the entry was made and initialled by the officer of the watch." Bullivant did not wait for Hamilton's confirmation. "So the fact that the entries after 14-03 were in the captain's handwriting would not be unusual?"

"No, sir."

Sir Abel looked complacently content as he dovetailed the final link in his chain of facts into place. Pausing to create the right atmosphere of suspense he played his trump card.

"In view of the evidence—the entries in the logbook and your own statements made under oath—do you not agree that, had you been aware of Lieutenant Commander Cavendish's real motive in carrying out this so-called attack, you would not have made your formal complaint."

Hamilton hesitated. He *knew* exactly what had happened that day and he could not understand how Bullivant had twisted the facts so effectively. There was only one answer he could make to the question in the form in which it was posed. And that answer would bring Cavendish's acquittal. He might receive a severe reprimand to keep the Germans happy, but that was all. And in a few month's time his career would flourish again. As he prepared to answer the question Hamilton realized bitterly that he had been cornered into confirming Gerry's preposterous defense.

"Given knowledge of the facts which you have explained to the court," he said slowly, "I agree I would not have lodged a complaint, sir."

Bullivant bowed to the president. It was a pity the lieutenant had been such an easy nut to crack. Another day of cross-examination would have earned him a further 500 guineas. Still he mustn't be too greedy. Anyway he was due in the Central Criminal Court at the Old Bailey on Friday, to defend the triple wife murderer Herbert Glossen.

"No more questions, Mr. President."

Davidge-Pitts looked enquiringly at Captain Dalby. "Do you wish to re-examine the witness?"

The prosecutor stood up, glanced quickly at Bullivant as he fluffed out his gown and sat down beside his client, and walked across the steel-decked courtroom.

"When did you last see the logbook, Lieutenant?"

"When I took it to the flagship and handed it to

Rear Admiral Robertson. That would be at about six o'clock the same evening."

"And you have not seen it since?"

"No sir."

"Did you inspect the entries before you took the log to the flagship, Lieutenant?"

"Yes, sir. I wanted to refresh my memory in case the commander-in-chief asked any questions."

"And what was the last entry when the log passed out of your custody?"

Bullivant leaned forward attentively to hear Hamilton's reply.

"The entry which I had made at 14-03 recording the submarine's time of diving, sir."

Dalby asked the deputy judge advocate for the logbook, opened it, and passed it to Hamilton.

"The entry at 14-03 is in your handwriting?"

"Yes, sir. I initialled it as officer of the watch."

"And these later entries—the entries relating to the German destroyers—in whose handwriting are they made?"

Hamilton looked down at the opened logbook. "They are in Liutenant Commander Cavendish's writing, sir."

The prosecutor nodded, took the logbook from Hamilton, and passed it back to the deputy judge advocate.

"Where was the logbook normally kept?" he asked casually.

"On a small table alongside the main blowing and venting panel."

"Alongside your station when the Attack Team is closed up, in fact."

"That is correct, sir."

"So I assume that it was within your view at all times."

"Yes, sir."

"Did the captain, or anyone else, maintain a rough log while the submarine was closed up for action?"

"No, sir. Lieutenant Commander Cavendish said that a rough log was a duplication of effort and we had too much paperwork to contend with in any case."

48

Dalby paused dramatically. The Court-martial Board could see where his cross-examination was leading and the vast hangar-deck throbbed with tension as he put his final question.

"So, Lieutenant Hamilton, as I understand it, the 14-03 entry was the final entry in the logbook when you handed it to Rear Admiral Robertson. And these subsequent entries—in which my learned friend has shown such great interest—were not written up at six o'clock that evening. Just one last question, Lieutenant. Did you see *anyone* make an entry in that log between 14-03 and the time *Surge* surfaced after the attack?"

"No, sir. I can swear that neither Lieutenant Commander Cavendish nor anyone else went near the log-book."

"Thank you. I have no more questions, Mr. President."

Davidge-Pitts looked across at Bullivant. Sir Abel had lost the smug smile. He turned and consulted his client in a whisper. Then he looked up at the president and shook his head.

"No more questions."

"If that's British justice then all I can say is—God help us!"

Commander Knight emptied his glass and quickly replaced it with another. Getting blind stinking drunk seemed to be the only solution.

"Absolutely, old boy," Blackhouse drawled. "I mean to say—how the devil are we going to field a polo team for the army match next month without Gerry Cavendish. They ought to consider these things in Whitehall, you know," he added in all seriousness.

"To hell with your bloody polo team, Blackie," Knight snapped as he started on his sixth pink gin of the evening. As the senior submarine commander in the wardroom he considered himself above such petty matters as polo matches. "What bothers me is the fact that there's going to be a bloody war inside twelve months and we need experienced skippers like Gerry."

"Not if he does damned silly things like trying to torpedo the German fleet before it's declared,"

49

Jameson said drily. He looked out from the circle of drinkers grouped around the bar. "Don't you agree, Nick?"

Hamilton did not want to get drawn into the discussion. He was convinced in his own mind that his damning evidence about the logbook had turned the scales against his former skipper. And he had not yet come to terms with his conscience. In addition he had a strong suspicion that the wardroom regarded him as responsible for the verdict.

"I don't know," he shrugged. "But Gerry was a bloody fine skipper, whatever his other faults might have been."

"I hear you didn't help much," Blackhouse observed bitterly. "Someone told me it was your evidence that's hung him. I'd hate to have a first officer who goes running to the flotilla commander each time I did something wrong."

Hamilton reddened and there was an embarrassed silence as the other officers studied their glasses with painstaking care in an effort to escape meeting his eyes.

"Don't be such a bloody idiot, Blackie," Commander Knight said sharply. "The court-martial was *in camera*, so no one knows what evidence was presented. And no one's likely to either. Hamilton was called upon to say his piece just the same as everyone else. He can't be blamed for what happened."

"Take no notice of Blackie, Nick," Windrush grinned. "He's more worried about his damned polo team than he is about Cavendish. Come on, cheer up, what'll you have?"

"Thanks, John. Just a small scotch, please." Hamilton realized that there was no escape. Perhaps it was better to get it all over and done with as soon as possible.

"The thing that shattered me was the sentence," the commander continued, while Windrush left the group to order Nick's drink. "I mean we *all* expected Gerry to be found guilty. But to sling him out of the service . . ."

"I wonder what he'll do now," Windrush asked as

he passed Hamilton his glass. "It won't be easy finding a new berth."

"I'm not so worried about that aspect." Commander Knight started on his seventh pink gin with the same eager relish he had shown toward the first. "Gerry's got plenty of money. He doesn't need to work. I'm more concerned that he'll do something stupid. We all know what a lunatic he can be when he feels like it."

. Hamilton was of the same opinion but he preferred to keep his private thoughts to himself. Despite his failings Cavendish had been a first-class shipmate and in many ways the two men had been as close as brothers. And, like Knight, he was concerned that, freed from the restraints of naval discipline, Gerry would get himself into serious trouble.

"I daresay he'll go off to Germany." Macauley, skipper of the S-class submarine *Serendipity,* had not joined in the conversation previously. Like Hamilton he regarded Cavendish as a friend who needed protecting from himself; he'd known him since they'd been term mates at Dartmouth in 1927. "Most of his family live over there and he speaks the lingo like a native."

"I'm sure you're right, sir," Blackhouse agreed. He was Macauley's first officer and his natural sycophancy was a constant irritation both to his friends and his more casual companions. "I must say I'm surprised his friends didn't put pressure on Hitler to hush the whole thing up—I believe they're very influential."

"To be honest," Knight admitted reluctantly, "that's the one thing that worries me more than anything else about Gerry. How the hell a chap with his background can admire these Nazi thugs is beyond me. He's the complete opposite of everything Hitler stands for."

"I don't think he really sympathizes with the Nazi movement," Hamilton interposed in defense of his friend. "I don't hold with Hitler's ideas any more than you do, but most of us have been to Germany recently and I think we're all agreed he's done wonders for his country. Personally I don't take too much notice of Gerry's opinion. He knows he gets up people's noses by boosting Hitler so he does it just for the hell of it."

51

"Perhaps," Macauley nodded doubtfully. "But it's lost him a lot of friends and I reckon it went against him at the court-martial." He looked around the circle. "My turn in the chair, I think. What are you chaps having?"

"Nothing for me, thanks, Peter," Hamilton excused himself. "I want to go along and say goodbye to Gerry. I believe he's leaving first thing tomorrow."

"Good idea, Nick. We'll all come along. I reckon a party is just what he needs at the moment."

Hamilton shook his head. "Sorry, Peter, but I'd rather see him on my own. I know I only told the truth at the court-martial but I'd like to make sure he understands. I'd hate there to be any ill-feeling."

"You can go on ahead, Hamilton." As the senior officer present Commander Knight took it upon himself to act as spokesman for the others. "We'll come along later. See you in an hour or so."

It was a warm evening and as Hamilton walked across the parade ground of Fort Blockhouse he could feel a soft south-westerly breeze blowing in from the sea across the ramparts. He paused for a moment and looked out over the Solent. The lights of a transatlantic liner coming down from Southampton en route to New York twinkled brightly against the dark mass of the Isle of Wight and, further to the east, under the shadow of the Nab Tower, three Home Fleet destroyers were returning to Portsmouth at the end of a day's anti-submarine exercises in the Channel.

Hamilton stopped by the sea wall to light his pipe. And as he watched the destroyers he realized with a shock that his next period of big-ship time was almost due. Like all officers in the submarine service he was required to spend a certain period as a watch-keeper between submarine appointments, and in common with all stalwarts of the trade he hated this enforced separation from his own branch of the service. The senseless petty restrictions of big-ship life irritated him beyond measure and he missed the friendly comradeship of the submarine service.

Apart from a few key ratings most watch-keeping officers knew only the men in their own division and, on a really big ship like *Leviathan,* even some of their fellow officers in the wardroom remained nameless strangers. After the intimate companionship of a submarine where an officer knew the first name of every single man aboard, and where discipline was not imposed but grew out of mutual respect and responsibility, life on a battleship was boring, fruitless and friendless.

But if he wanted to get selected for the "perisher" a change of routine was vital. Reports by post-captains in command of battleships and battle-cruisers carried considerably more weight than those submitted by the new lieutenant commanders who skippered most submarines. And a good report from the right man at the right time could make all the difference in the difficult task of obtaining a command appointment.

The liner was already fading from view as it passed the Foreland. And he could see the regular flash from the lighthouse at Bembridge Point as the great ship steamed south-east at a steady 20 knots. Pausing for a moment to light his pipe again Hamilton watched the destroyers swing to starboard to keep the Spit Sands Fort on their port beams as they began their final approach toward the narrow entrance to the dockyard at the Sallyport. It was a moonless night and the colored lights of the fairground behind Clarence Pier stood out in bright contrast to the darkened destroyers moving like deep shadows on the blackness of the sea.

As he watched the three destroyers feeling their way cautiously into harbor Hamilton sensed that war was very close. Hitler was already threatening the independence of Czechoslovakia and if events moved at their usual pace he expected to see a conflagration in Central Europe by October at the latest. After the hideous sacrifices of the Great War it seemed almost incredible that now, in 1938, just twenty years after the Armistice, Europe was once again hovering on the brink of another suicidal holocaust.

He turned away from the ramparts and started across the asphalt toward the officers' quarters.

Cavendish's cabin—in true navy fashion the four-square brick-built rooms were still given their nautical title—was on the first floor and Hamilton wondered what sort of welcome he would receive. Cavendish had rewarded him with a hard searching look when he had finally stepped down from the witness stand but it was difficult to judge what thoughts lay behind those bland blue eyes. But Hamilton was not one to shirk a self-imposed duty for fear of the consequences. He knocked on the door.

"Come in, it's not locked. And don't fall over the bloody suitcases!"

It was a timely warning. Three large pigskin cases, a bag of well-used golf clubs, and a battered brass-bound sea chest stood immediately behind the door. Hamilton picked his way over them carefully.

"What ho, Nick! Good of you to come over. Find yourself a chair while I dig out a bottle."

Cavendish's civilian clothes looked strangely out of place against the familiar background of his comfortable little room. He seemed none the worse for the court-martial verdict and was grinning widely.

"I won't have a drink at the moment, thanks, Gerry." Hamilton looked around at the chaos of clothes, cases, mementoes, and sporting equipment littering the cabin. "I only dropped in to say I'm sorry . . . and to wish you luck."

"Don't look so damned miserable, old boy. I got what I asked for and I only hold myself to blame. If I'd listened to you in the first place I wouldn't be in this bloody mess now."

"But my official complaint didn't exactly help."

Cavendish threw some tennis rackets into a large canvas holdall and laughed easily. "Look, Nick, you're an old duffer. Stop worrying about it. You did exactly what the book said. And you had the guts to stick to your guns against a lot of opposition." He rummaged through a pile of clothing in search of some tennis balls. "There were certain people in high places who wouldn't rest until they'd had me slung out. They're the villains of the piece—not you." He fell back into a chair with a sigh and reached for a bottle of gin.

"What do you intend doing now?" Hamilton asked.

"To be honest I'm not really sure. I've been invited

down to Cannes by Dolores." Cavendish's name had often been linked with film star Dolores Velequez by newspaper gossip columnists." But I reckon a fortnight of dear little Dotty's home comforts will be all that flesh and blood can stand. I did think of trying one of the South American navies but there's plenty of time for that later. So I've decided to have a crack at motor racing for a couple of seasons and see how I get on if I take it seriously."

"What are you aiming at—a place in one of the works teams like Seaman!"*

"Poor old Dick. He and I were at school together, you know. We used to play truant and go to Brooklands." Cavendish poured himself a drink and scratched his head thoughtfully. "Actually I *was* thinking along those lines, Nick. I've put the old Alvis up for sale and I've ordered one of the new 16-valve Maseratis from Italy. Camponi is going to prepare it for me and I'm entering in every *voiturette* event I can manage. With a bit of luck, and if I do well enough, I might get a test drive for one of the factory teams."

"A German team of course?" Hamilton knew it was a silly question. The Mercedes Benz and Auto Union teams, liberally backed by Nazi finance, completely dominated the Grand Prix circuits. But he was curious to see Cavendish's reaction.

"I don't see why not," he shrugged. "No one complained when Dick was given a team place with Mercedes. And as my cousin has a *schloss* a few miles out of Stuttgart it would certainly be convenient."

"Well, the best of luck. If I get a chance I'll come along and watch you. Let me know when you're racing and I'll try to fix it in with my leave."

"Great! But there's no reason why we shouldn't get together before then—the season doesn't start until April. How about coming down to Norfolk for a spot of sailing next month?"

*Richard Seaman, a wealthy young English amateur racing driver, was given a place in the German Mercedes Benz team in 1937. He won the German Grand Prix but was killed in Belgium a few weeks after his triumph.

Cavendish was a keen amateur yachtsman and Hamilton had crewed for him on numerous occasions. Gerry's happy hunting ground was along the east coast of England and he was almost unbeatable in his home waters. He knew the tides, the currents, and the shifting sandbanks like the back of his hand and few were expert enough to match him when he had the bit between his teeth.

Hamilton thoroughly enjoyed his weekends on Cavendish's racing yacht *Merle* and it had not taken him long to pick up the rudimentary techniques of sail and rope handling. Having been promoted from the lower deck he lacked Gerry's youthful experience with the sailing cutters at Dartsmouth Naval College but Cavendish was a good instructor and together they made a first class team.

But for all his expertise there was little doubt that Cavendish's success stemmed mainly from his intimate knowledge of the treacherous coastal waters of East Anglia. There had been many occasions when he had proved the charts of the area to be incorrect. Winds and tides could cut deep passages through the sandbanks where, only a few days earlier, there had been insufficient depth of water for even a dinghy to pass through. And he made good use of his uncanny local knowledge when he planned his racing strategy.

"Count me in any time," Hamilton accepted eagerly. "Is there anything special on?"

"It's the last race in the series for the Admiral's Trophy. *Merle*'s already ahead on points and I'm dying to beat old Toby, the club commodore." He glanced up at the wall calendar. "It's on September 12. Can you make a note in your diary?"

"I thought you were going down to Cannes with Dolores," Hamilton reminded him. The 12th was only a week ahead.

"So I am—but I'll be back by then. Even Dotty's delectable little fanny won't be enough to keep me away. In any case," he added inconsequentially, "I always keep a bit of spare tucked away near home for a rainy day. Remind me to introduce you to Caroline. She's only eighteen but I'll bet she's opened her legs more times than Tower Bridge. You'll enjoy her. In both senses of the word."

"Thanks for the offer, Gerry, but I'd rather spend my weekend on *Merle*."

"It's up to you, old boy. Personally I'd rather spend mine on Caroline—she's a bloody sight more comfortable than an unsprung bunk." Cavendish tilted the glass and finished his drink. "Right! If you catch the 9.12 from King's Cross I can pick you up at King's Lynn and drive you back to Framlingham."

Hamilton got out of his chair. "Fine, I'll be there." He held out his hand. "Good luck, Gerry. And for Christ's sake look after yourself." He flushed slightly. "We're all a bit worried about you."

"Don't worry, Nick, I intend to." Cavendish grabbed his hand and squeezed it firmly. "I don't propose writing myself off at the tender age of thirty-two. And don't blame yourself for what's happened. You did exactly what any responsible officer would have done in the circumstances. And I wouldn't have wanted it any other way."

"Okay, see you at King's Lynn station on Saturday week." Hamilton opened the door, hesitated for a moment, and then turned. There was a broad grin on his normally serious face. "And you'd better get Caroline warmed up ready for me. I always did enjoy watching Tower Bridge in action."


# CHAPTER FOUR

"Main motors grouped down and ready, sir."

"Thank you, Number One." Hamilton bent over the voicepipe. "Obey telegraphs." He waited for the acknowledgement and straightened up. "Let go aft, Number One! Let go for'ard!"

Despite all the appearances of outward calm Hamilton felt his heart beat a shade faster as *Rapier* came under his command for the first time. Moving to the conning-tower rails he watched the deck party on the fore-casing release the securing wires and let them drop into the turgid water of the fitting-out basin with a splash.

"Starboard 30, Cox'n."

*Rapier* was moored with her bows pointing toward the open gates of the dock and, for the moment at least, Hamilton was spared the nerve-racking task of maneuvering a new and untried submarine in the narrow confines of the shipyard basin.

"Slow ahead starboard."

The ting-ting of the telegraph repeater echoed faintly from the motor room deep down inside the steel bowels of the submarine as the order was received and executed.

"Starboard motor going ahead, sir."

Hamilton glanced instinctively at the stern. A gentle ripple trembled on the surface of the muddy water and, as the starboard propeller began to revolve, the tiny ripples grew into miniature waves. His face was impassive as he watched the gray stone wall of the dock gliding slowly astern as *Rapier* got under way. He waited until the fantail was clear.

"Port 30, Cox'n. Stop starboard motor. Steady . . ."

Swinging slowly under the momentum of her weight *Rapier* responded obediently to the helm. The submarine's blunt bows lined up with the dock gates like the sights of a rifle coming on target and Hamilton nodded.

"Midships helm. Slow ahead together. She's all yours, Cox'n. Take her through the middle."

Hamilton leaned his elbows on the edge of the bridge coaming and stared ahead as he savored the moment. *Rapier* was his third command since his graduation from the "perisher" course at Fort Blockhouse at the beginning of 1939. And, as a brand-new boat, she was his proudest.

*H-79,* a relic of the 1914–18 war, had been his first command appointment on leaving Blockhouse. But despite a natural affection for her antique crankiness, she was long past her prime. And as a prudent precaution the flotilla commander had limited her maximum diving depth to ten fathoms. Captain (S) obviously had no great faith in either him or the boat—but Hamilton was never quite sure which. *H-79* had been succeeded by *L-76,* another First World War veteran—a ponderous sulky brute of a beast. He was not sorry when the commission ended and she was struck off the active list.

The Munich crisis of October, 1938, quickly brought the Royal Navy to war readiness and, in the process, exposed many of the organizational defects that had been hidden by the long years of peace and retrenchment. Most important, so far as Hamilton was concerned, was the discovery that the new submarines ordered by Parliament under the Emergency War Program found the Royal Navy woefully short of trained submarine commanders. As a result his projected transfer to watch-keeping duties on the battleship *Royal Oak* was hurriedly canceled on the direct orders of the flag officer (submarines) and he was selected for the Commanding Officer's Qualifying Course.*

*Rapier* cleared the dock gates and her freshly painted bows thrust into the Clyde.

"Starboard 15!"

Chief Petty Officer Ernie Blood, coxswain of *Rapier* and the senior non-commissioned officer on board, echoed the order and spun the wheel on to the new course. Like most of the crew he was curious to judge the skill of their new skipper—and his temper. Although no details of the court-martial had escaped from the shroud of secrecy which the admiralty had drawn over the evidence, it was common knowledge among the Lower Deck that Hamilton had been first officer to Cavendish on *Surge.* Like most British sailors they were fair minded and Hamilton would get an adequate chance to prove himself. But they were watching him closely.

"In both clutches. Switches off."

Now that *Rapier* was in the open river and the need for delicate maneuvering was no longer necessary, Hamilton went over to the submarine's main diesel engines in order to prevent any further drain on the bat-

---

* Hamilton was, in fact, doubly lucky. *Royal Oak* was torpedoed and sunk on October 14, 1939, with the loss of over 800 lives when the German U-boat ace Gunther Prien made a daring surface attack on the fleet anchorage at Scapa Flow.

teries and to conserve electric power. Out of the corner of his eye he could see Cox'n Blood nod approvingly to himself as he heard the order and concluded with some satisfaction, that in the veteran's expert experience, he had judged the correct moment for the change-over.

"How is she, Mr. Hamilton?"

Harry Duncan, the Assistant Managing Director of Fairchild & Chandler Ltd., loked strangely out of place on the exposed bridge of the submarine in his civilian clothes. And the square set black bowler hat added a touch of comedy to his precise appearance. *Rapier,* officially, was still *Job No 738.* She would not become one of His Majesty's ships until the acceptance trials were completed and Hamilton had signed the formal handing-over documents. And until that moment the submarine remained the property of her builders, Fairchild & Chandler Ltd.

"Handles like a dream, Mr. Duncan," Hamilton told him. "Are your men settled in down below?"

Specialists from the shipyard normally sailed on acceptance trials to observe the submarine's performance and to advise on unexpected technical problems. But since the loss of the *Thetis* the previous month* during her acceptance trials in Liverpool Bay few shipyard civilians were enthusiastic about going to sea with a new and untested submarine. It was obvious from the expressions on the men's faces when they came aboard that they were uneasy. But, as Hamilton had anticipated, they soon lost their initial fears as they settled down in the cheerful company of *Rapier*'s extrovert and confident crew members.

"They're fine," Duncan confirmed. Turning up the collar of his raincoat, he watched the shrouded banks of the Clyde slide past in the early morning mists. *Mistral,* their escort tug, would be waiting off Garroch Head and she would mother the submarine south and west to the diving area. "Weren't you with Mr. Cavendish on the *Surge,* sir?"

Hamilton nodded. He wondered how Duncan knew

* *Thetis* sank on June 1, 1939. There were only three survivors and, in addition to the submarine's crew, 33 civilian shipyard workers lost their lives.

about Gerry Cavendish. He'd probably read about it in the newspapers and was hoping to pick up some gossip. Well, he was going to be unlucky.

"Yes, I served with Lieutenant Commander Cavendish," he said shortly. "I was his first officer."

Duncan wagged his head sententiously. "It's a small world, Lieutenant. His family are the majority shareholders in our company, you know. I've met him several times. He's got a seat on the board. Non-executive, of course."

Hamilton was listening with only half an ear. *Rapier* was passing Gourock on its port hand and the red warning flags were up to indicate torpedo trials in progress at the Royal Navy Torpedo factory. He raised his binoculars and searched the river ahead as it broadened into its confluence with Loch Long and Holy Loch. The morning ferry was crossing from Dunoon but it would be safely clear by the time they intersected its track and he anticipated no difficulties although he ordered a reduction in speed as a precaution.

"Take over, Mr. Collis," he told *Rapier*'s first officer. "I'll relieve you when we reach Toward light." He turned back to Duncan. "I'm sorry. What were you saying just now?"

"I said that Lieutenant Commander Cavendish is a member of our board of directors. In fact I saw him last month."

"How's he getting on? I haven't seen him since we won the Admiral's Trophy last year. I gather he's still motor-racing."

"Aye, that's right enough," Duncan nodded. "The silly young fool will kill himself one of these days. Mind you, though, he's doing very well."

"Can't say I follow the sport myself," Hamilton admitted, "although it's impossible to miss seeing his name in the newspapers every time he wins something. Any idea what he's doing next month—I've got some leave coming up and I promised to go along and watch one of his races."

Despite the Scotsman's dourness it was plain that

61

Duncan, like most people who came into contact with Cavendish, had fallen under his spell.

"He told me he'd be at Crystal Palace for the Esso Cup in July. Then he's off to Germany to test drive for one of their teams. I think he said Mercedes-Benz."

"Well I hope he makes it," Hamilton said sincerely. "Team discipline would do him good. And I know he's set his heart on a place in one of the big factory teams." He glanced astern to make sure *Rapier* had passed clear of the torpedo testing range. "Shall we go down to the wardroom, Mr. Duncan? I've still one or two matters to check with your chief engineer."

*Rapier*'s wardroom was cramped enough at the best of times but with three civilian engineers, the admiralty superintendent, Commander Lewis, two officers from flotilla acting as observers, and the submarine's own engineering officer, Sean O'Brien, it resembled the Black Hole of Calcutta. And the arrival of Duncan and the skipper did little to improve the overcrowded conditions.

"Any problems so far?" Hamilton asked Jackson, the senior of the shipyard's engineers and the man responsible for the blowing and venting gear.

"Everything's fine, Lieutenant. But I'd like to do a vacuum test before the first dive."

Hamilton looked up sharply. "Any reason, Mr. Jackson?"

The engineer shook his head. "No—just put it down to the fact that I'm a canny Scot. I'd rather be safe than sorry."

"She performed to my satisfaction when we carried out the initial diving tests in the fitting-out basin," Commander Lewis intervened. He turned to the submarine's engineering officer for confirmation.

"To be sure she did," O'Brien agreed in a broad Irish accent. "But a dockyard basin isn't after having much pressure of water. About the only thing you find out is that she's not leaking like a sieve."

"I should hope *not*, Mr. Engineer," Duncan said coldly. Every new submarine placed his company's reputation on the block until it had been tried, tested, and

62

passed, and he did not appreciate the navy's sense of humor.

"Nevertheless," Hamilton said grimly, "I'm none too happy about the trim." As skipper of *Rapier* he bore the ultimate responsibility. And if anything were to go wrong he would have to shoulder the blame. He opened one of the files and spread out a set of carefully typed figures on the wardroom table. The other men leaned forward to see them. "According to my interpretation of these," he said, "she seems a couple of inches lighter in the bows than when you tested her in the fitting-out basin. To be completely frank, and with no disrespect to your engineers, Mr. Duncan, I've got reservations about the trim you've put on her."

"I don't think you have anything to worry about, Lieutenant. We can always flood up a couple of the bow torpedo tubes to compensate."

"I don't like the idea," Hamilton told him brusquely.

"Neither do I," Commander Lewis agreed. As the admiralty overseer he had supervised more than twenty trials and he probably knew more about submarines than any other man aboard. "But, on the other hand, this job's already three months late because of the strike at the yard at Christmas. And I don't think the admiralty will welcome a further delay. It's your responsibility, of course, Lieutenant Hamilton. My rank does not count in these circumstances. But I would be ignoring my duty if I did not draw your attention to the admiralty's views."

"Is this why you want the vacuum test, Mr. Jackson?" Hamilton asked the civilian engineer pointedly.

Jackson hesitated. "Partially," he admitted reluctantly. "But I'm quite happy with the trim. It was just a routine safety precaution. You can't be too careful after . . ." He did not need to finish the sentence. Everyone knew he was thinking of the *Thetis* disaster.

Hamilton stared down at the figures. As Jackson had pointed out, the degree of lightness was extremely small and was probably due to no more than the fact that one of the trimming tanks was empty when, according to the gauge, it was full. It could be put right easily once *Rapier* returned to the dockyard and it would have no effect on the submarine's performance. And, as Lewis had reminded him, if he delayed the diving trials the whole commissioning program would be set back by a week or more. *Rapier* was urgently required to replace an *R-class* boat going out to the Far East to reinforce the China Fleet against Japanese war threats and any delay would upset a large number of carefully drawn interlocking ship movements. Duncan was quite right. If the bows were too light they could always flood up the tubes and restore trim by using them as auxiliary ballast tanks. It had been done before.

*"Captain to the bridge. Toward light one mile distant on starboard bow."*

Hamilton closed the file and reached for his cap. The conference was over and it was time to take the decision. The lives of over 40 men rested in his hands and he was conscious of the responsibility. Notwithstanding Lewis's senior rank and Jackson's greater experience of submarine construction, the ultimate decision had to be his—and his alone.

"The acceptance trials will continue, gentlemen," he told the experts quietly. "Stand by to put on the vacuum test in an hour. And you'd best flood up Numbers 5 and 6 tubes. I'll need as near perfect trim as I can get for the first dive."

Sliding the curtain to one side he stepped out into the narrow corridor that ran down the fore-and-aft axis of the submarine and made his way into the control room.

*HMS Rapier,* despite the initial letter of her name, was one of the highly successful "S" class submarines designed for medium range patrols in confined waters. Her home station would be the North Sea and she was the first of a repeat batch of a tried and tested design—*Swordfish,* nameship of the class, had been launched in 1931—which had been hurriedly placed on order by the Admiralty in 1938 to release the larger "P" and "R" boats for the overseas flotillas.

Displacing 765 tons on the surface at full load she could take on 290 tons of water ballast for diving and she measured a fraction under 209 feet from nose to tail with a maximum beam of 24 feet. Not that the crew enjoyed such spaciousness, for over half the vessel's width was taken up by the great bulging ballast tanks, so they were confined to a narrow tube of steel that was never more than 12 feet across at its widest.

The two 8-cylinder admiralty-pattern diesels drove her at a maximum speed of 13.75 knots in surface trim while, for underwater running, her 1,550 BHP electric motors pushed her through the depths at up to 10 knots although such relatively high speed was reserved for emergencies only. Her maximum diving depth of 300 feet was enough to escape depth-charge attacks and the six 21″ torpedo tubes packed into her bows made her more than a match for even the mightiest battleship that might chance to cross her path.

Hamilton was already proud of his tiny yet devastatingly destructive command. And despite a natural concern about trim he sensed she was a tight little boat which would amply repay his confidence in her when the time came. And, he reflected, as the crew cleared the conning-tower in readiness for the vacuum test, the time when that destructive power would be unleashed seemed to be fast approaching. Prime Minister Chamberlain may have sold out to Hitler at Munich the previous year but it was clear that any further demands by the German dictator would meet with a stern rebuff from both Britain and France. And Hitler's speeches against Poland suggested that war would engulf Europe in the near future. Within a few months he had little doubt that *Rapier* would be hunting the North Sea in earnest.

"All hands below, sir."

Hamilton acknowledged the report and moved to the voicepipe connecting the bridge to the control room below. "Secure upper and lower hatches, Number One. You may proceed with the vacuum test as soon as you're ready."

He replaced the watertight cover on the voicepipe and closed the cock carefully. The blasting roar of the diesels suddenly died away as the main engines were stopped and he could feel the hull plates gently vibrating as the electric motors took over. He experienced a

65

strange sensation of isolation and loneliness. Only the cox'n, Ernie Blood, and the yeoman signaler remained with him on the empty bridge; the battened hatches had now cut them off completely from their shipmates inside the hull. Keeping a watchful eye out for approaching surface vessels Hamilton rested his elbows on the conning-tower coaming and waited.

Inside *Rapier* the air compressors were left running for a few moments after the hatches were clipped—normally they were shut off before diving—and the air pressure mounted quickly. It was like descending in a high-speed lift and the men swallowed hard to equalize the uncomfortable pressure on their eardrums. Collis watched the needle of the barometer climb and, as it reached critical pressure, he nodded to Tropp, the submarine's second coxswain.

"Compressor's off!"

It was now just a matter of waiting, watching and listening. With every seam and hatchway under pressure from within the submarine any serious leaks would be quickly audible to the trained ear. And the crew, backed by dockyard technicians, listened carefully at all the known points of weakness—the lower conning-tower hatch, the engine room exhaust baffles, the torpedo-loading hatch in the fore-ends and, right forward in the narrow confines of the bow compartment, the rear doors of the six torpedo tubes.

Jackson's fears, however, proved groundless. No serious leaks were reported and at the end of five minutes there had been no drop in the level of barometric pressure. Collis checked his watch to ensure that the full test time had elapsed and pulled the cock from the control-room end of the bridge voicepipe.

Hamilton heard the sudden rush of released air and turned as Maitland unfastened the clips of the upper hatch and swung open the heavy steel cover. The build-up of pressure tore the heavy lid from his hand and it swung back on its hinge to strike the deck plating with a loud clatter. Having undone the hatch, Maitland slid back down the ladder and, a moment later, Collis poked his head up through the oval-shaped opening.

"Vacuum test completed, sir," he reported a trifle unnecessarily. "Pressure maintained. No leaks, sir."

Hamilton nodded. He had not expected there to be any. And if there had been he'd have had Duncan's head on a platter without delay. "Thank you, Number One. Stand by for diving in five minutes."

Collis disappeared down the ladder and Hamilton moved to the voicepipe to begin the diving routine. In combat conditions *Rapier* would dive in thirty seconds. Not *crash* dive—submariners did not recognize such an expression. They left that sort of thing to fiction writers who could not accept the calm unhurried efficiency of a trained submarine crew working under combat conditions. But on this initial trim dive Hamilton intended to take things at a careful and leisurely pace. Everything had to be double-checked and independently tested; for, except in the artificial surroundings of the shallow dockyard basin, *Job No 738* had never been beneath the surface before. And in the cold depths of the Firth of Clyde there could be no room for error.

"Control room! Stand by to take over lower steering."

*Rapier* had been steered down the Clyde from the upper bridge position by the first coxswain. But when the submarine went to diving stations his place was at the controls of the aft hydroplanes and he needed time to get below to take up his allotted post.

"Ready to take over lower steering, sir."

"Take over lower steering. Course 1-9-0."

"Lower steering taken over, sir. Steady on 1-9-0."

"Are the towing buffs ready, Yeoman?"

Chief Petty Officer Drury checked the lashings of the grass line and its three orange buoys and handed it to Truman—one of the leading seamen the skipper had called to the bridge. "Aye, aye, sir."

"Stream the buffs! And run the red flag up the periscope, Yeoman."

The orange colored buoys bobbing on the surface when the submarine submerged would act as a guide to the escorting tug and the grass line was plenty long enough to reach the surface even when the vessel was on the bottom. The red flag was the standard warning signal that the submarine was about to dive.

"Yeoman! Call up *Mistral*. Make: DIVING IN FIVE MINUTES. SPEED FOUR KNOTS. DURATION OF DIVE TEN MINUTES. REPEAT TO DOLPHIN."

Drury tucked the Aldis lamp into his shoulder, sighted on *Mistral*'s bridge, and began to flash the message. Within minutes of its receipt the escort tug's powerful radio would be transmitting *Rapier*'s time of diving and surfacing to the duty signal officer at *HMS Dolphin* so that the information could be duly logged. In peacetime every submarine was required to report to *Dolphin* stating its position, time of diving, and estimated position and time of resurfacing. And if the submarine failed to reappear on the surface at the time given, the Royal Navy's nerve-center at Fort Blockhouse immediately alerted all emergency services near the submarine's last known position to stand by for a possible disaster.

A reply flickered from *Mistral*'s bridge and Drury mouthed the letters as he read them off.

"Signal from *Mistral,* sir. Reads: GOOD LUCK STOP WET THE BABY'S HEAD FOR ME."

Hamilton grinned and waved his arm at Lieutenant James who was acting as official observer aboard the tug.

"All hands to diving stations! Clear the bridge! Stand by to dive!"

The men on the bridge made their way unhurriedly down the conning-tower ladder and, after a final glance around the horizon, Hamilton pushed the diving klaxon and swung his legs into the open hatch. Reaching upwards he pulled the heavy cover shut, pushed the clips securely into place and inserted the safety pins.

"Upper hatch closed. Clips in. Pins secured."

Having reported the standard routine—a normal precaution for diving exercises in peacetime—he continued down the ladder, passed through the lower conning-tower compartment, and jumped the last few feet into the control room. Able Seaman Wharr closed the lower hatch and intoned the ritual: "Lower hatch secured. Clips on, sir."

The control room reeked of fresh paint. The familiar

68

submarine smell of sour cabbage, sweat, dampness and diesel oil had not, as yet, had time to build up and pollute the atmosphere. Hamilton moved to the center of the crowded compartment.

"Up periscope!"

The large bi-focal navigation 'scope slid smoothly from its well and Hamilton pushed his face into the rubber mask shielding the delicate lenses of the binocular eye-piece. With *Rapier* still running on the surface he had a literal bird's eye view of the sea and he tilted the upper lens so that he could look down at the submarine's bows.

"Test hydroplanes. Turn out fore-planes."

Bill Tropp, *Rapier*'s second coxswain, moved the large-diameter diving wheel and Hamilton watched the great steel fins unfold from their shielded nacelle just behind the bows like the rigid wings of a prehistoric bird opening in readiness for flight.

"Test fore and aft planes, Number One."

The fins moved up and down in response to Collis's instructions to the two coxswains and a few moments later he reported, "Hydroplanes tested and found correct, sir."

All pre-diving checks were now complete. The boat was leak-free, the 'planes were working, the pumps, airlines and blowing valves were functioning correctly. All that remained was the real thing.

Hamilton methodically checked off each warning light and gauge reading. Satisfied with what he had seen he turned to Fairchild & Chandler's senior representative for final clearance.

"Everything okay, Mr. Duncan?"

"Aye, Captain. She looks tight enough."

"Here we go then." He glanced at his watch to confirm that the diving time matched that given in his signal to *Mistral.* "Stop engines—clutches out. Switches on and group down. Motors slow ahead together." He paused cautiously for the acknowledgement. "Open main vents. Take her to 30 feet, Number One."

*Rapier* slid her bows gently into the sea as the hydroplanes tilted and, losing positive buoyancy as the water rushed into the empty ballast tanks, she slid quietly beneath the surface with the effortless ease of a diving porpoise. The lookout on *Mistral's* bridge noted the exact time of submergence on a slip of paper and handed it to a runner to take to the radio operator for transmission to Fort Blockhouse. And as the submarine vanished under the surface leaving only the questing tip of its periscope peeping coyly above the waves, Lieutenant James saw the orange buoys of the towing buff stream astern in the dying wash of her propellers.

The first five minutes of the trial had gone well and the tight lips of the civilian technicians gradually relaxed into satisfied smiles as Hamilton tested each item of equipment in turn and reported it to be correct.

"The trim seems right enough now, Number One," he observed to Collis, having completed a careful inspection of the inclinometer and depth gauges. "Did you flood up Numbers 5 and 6 tubes as instructed?"

"No, sir. I believe Mr. Duncan did."

"Aye, that's correct, Lieutenant," Duncan confirmed. "A couple of my lads looked after that wee job a couple of minutes after you mentioned it."

Hamilton nodded. It didn't matter to him who had actually carried out the flooding routine so long as the tubes were full. It was only later that he appreciated the full significance of Duncan's reply. He picked up the telephone linking the control room to the fore-ends. Sub-Lieutenant Martindale, the submarine's fourth hand and the man responsible for the bow torpedo compartment, answered it.

"Torpedo flat."

"This is the captain. Please check that both Number 5 and Number 6 tubes are flooded."

Martindale passed the request to leading Torpedoman Bates who squatted down behind the rear doors of the two lower torpedo tubes. He turned the inspection tap of Number 5 and a thin jet of water streamed out of the nozzle. Turning it off quickly he leaned across to Number 6 tube and repeated the routine. But this time nothing emerged from the tap. He moved the lever back into the "closed" position and, still squatting on his haunches, reported to Martindale over his shoulder.

70

"Number 5's flooded up, sir. But there's nothing coming out of No. 6."

Martindale turned back to the phone. "Torpedo flat reporting, sir. No. 5 is flooded out but No. 6 seems to be empty. Any instructions, sir?"

"No—maintain situation. Do nothing." Hamilton replaced the phone on its hook and frowned. If Martindale was correct it meant that the final set of trim figures were wrong. Picking up his slide rule he rechecked the data in the trim file. It was totally impossible to obtain a correct trim with only one of the tubes flooded if those figures were right—yet *Rapier* was trimmed perfectly according to the gauges. And that posed a difficult question. How could he accept *Job No 738* on behalf of His Majesty's Royal Navy while he still had doubts about her stability?

"Still worried about the trim, Hamilton?" He looked around and found Commander Lewis standing behind him. "She looks okay to me."

"I know. And that's the trouble. According to Martindale we've only got one tube flooded and that means the shipyard's final trim calculation is up the spout. If these figures are correct we should still be light by the bows."

Lewis shrugged. "So far as I'm concerned she's fine. You can see for yourself that the trim's perfect. If she goes back to the builders we won't see her again for another month."

"But surely it won't take more than a day or so to recheck the ballast calculation," Hamilton protested.

"I quite agree—but the yard's coming out on strike again tomorrow and the union is preparing for a long fight this time."

"Is that correct, Mr. Duncan?" Hamilton asked.

Duncan seemed reluctant to acknowledge the situation. Finally he nodded. "I'm afraid Commander Lewis is right, Lieutenant. If *Rapier* has to go back to the yard I doubt if you'll have her commissioned this side of Christmas."

Hamilton wondered bitterly what the nation would do if the navy decided to go on strike too. Then he remembered the Invergordon Mutiny just eight years

71

earlier. It was no use the proverbial pot calling the kettle black. Recriminations were no help. Lewis was right. *Rapier*'s trim was perfect and he had no valid reason for refusing to sign the acceptance note on behalf of the admiralty. It was the unknown factor that worried him. A submarine should hold no secrets from her commander. And there was only one way to discover the answer.

"Down periscope! Take her down to 200 feet, Number One."

Lewis raised his eyebrows as he heard the order. It was against every rule in the book to take a submarine on a deep dive on her acceptance trials. But he could sympathize with Hamilton's decision. If *Rapier* could maintain her trim and stand up to the tremendous pressure of the sea at a depth of 200 feet there was clearly nothing very much wrong with her. But Hamilton was taking a hell of a gamble and Lewis secretly admired his guts.

The hull plates groaned under the pressure as the submarine leveled off at 200 feet and the two coxswains directed a sluggish response to the hydroplanes. However, a heaviness in the controls was not uncommon at these sort of depths and they saw no significance in the submarine's lazy obedience.

"Check all compartments for leaks, Number One."

Collis passed the order down the submarine and waited. Suddenly the green warning light blinked over the telephone link to the bow torpedo compartment and Hamilton felt his muscles tighten in anticipation of an unforeseen emergency. As he lifted the telephone he saw Duncan exchange a worried glance with Commander Lewis. Even the imperturbable Ernie Blood, sitting stolidly in front of the diving wheels, sucked his teeth thoughtfully. With the *Thetis* disaster so fresh in their minds, any suggestion of trouble in the fore-ends was sufficient to send cold shivers of fear down every spine.

"This is the captain. Report please."

"Martindale, sir. Shall I open the rear doors and inspect the bow caps for leaks?"

Hamilton, however, did not allow the anticlimax of

the request to lessen his caution. The mouth of each torpedo tube was sealed with a heavy watertight door which could be opened mechanically from inside the submarine and, provided the hollow tube was first pumped dry, it was possible for a torpedoman to crawl inside the narrow cylinder through the rear door to check the bow caps for leaks. It was a routine operation but he hesitated. Despite Duncan's platitudes and Lewis's assurances he remained convinced that *something* was wrong in the fore-ends and any attempt to open the rear loading doors of the torpedo tubes could be a recipe for disaster.

And yet, whether the risk were real or imaginary, he needed to have absolute confidence in his new command and it was no use running away . . .

The group of officers huddled on the starboard wing of *Mistral*'s bridge stared silently at the orange buoys bobbing in the rising swell. No one seemed to want to voice his inner thoughts. It was the tug's skipper, Baines, who finally spoke.

"She's a good five minutes overdue, Lieutenant. How much longer before we send a signal?"

As the Royal Navy's official observer, it was up to James to take the decision. *Mistral* was only on charter to the admiralty for the duration of the trials and Baines had no control over the matter. Unwilling to admit the possibility of disaster he shook his head and grasped at straws.

"We'll give them a little longer," he told the tug captain. "The buoys are still moving and if anything had gone wrong we'd have seen air bubbles on the surface."

"The buoys are drifting with the wind," Baines said unhelpfully. He was no submariner. But as a professional seaman he knew that every second wasted lessened the chances of survival if *Rapier*'s crew were trapped below. "And if the hull's intact, there won't be any air escaping to cause bubbles," he added pointedly.

Lieutenant James was in no mood to listen to dismal Jimmys. Inwardly he was as pessimistic as Baines. But he knew Hamilton well; they'd served together on several submarines, and it was inconceivable that anything could have happened to him. Even so the tub skipper was right about one thing—the lack of escaping air was inconclusive. A battery explosion could have killed everyone on board without fracturing the pressure hull. Or seawater coming into contact with the batteries might have filled the submarine with chlorine gas. Unwilling to accept the balance of probabilities he grasped at another straw.

"Even if you're right, Mr. Baines, I still don't accept that there's any trouble. *Rapier* would have sent up a marker buoy if she was in trouble."

Baines shrugged. Picking up his glasses, he searched the empty sea yet again. It was no use talking to a brick wall.

The men grouped on the bridge fell silent. Each had his own theory as to what might might have happened, but not one of them felt optimistic. Gripping the rails of the tug as it rolled and dipped in the swell, they stared out over the blank gray sea until their eyes were aching with the strain.

"Ten minutes, Lieutenant. She's ten minutes overdue now."

James pushed himself away from the rail like a punch-drunk boxer reeling from his corner at the sound of the bell. Digging into his pocket, the lieutenant pulled out a signal pad and a stump of pencil. He could feel his hands trembling as he began to draft the fatal message to Fort Blockhouse.

"Air bubbles on the surface! Two points off starboard bow!"

Thrusting the note-pad back into his pocket James hurried to the rails to join the tug's skipper and the other men crowded together on the starboard wing of the bridge. All eyes were searching anxiously to the south-east and it was Baines who located the spot first.

"Over there, Lieutenant!"

Giant bubbles of air rose to the surface and burst like pricked balloons with a sharp popping noise that was clearly audible to the men on *Mistral's* bridge. The water was boiling in a lather of white froth as if two primeval sea monsters were fighting a battle to the

74

death just below the surface and the rising wind ripped a spume of spray from the heaving tumult. Suddenly one of the sea monsters reared up and the black sheen of its rounded body glistened in the sun.

"It's *Rapier*!"

The submarine rolled gently as she emerged from the center of the maelstrom. Water streamed down her paintwork and cascaded from the drain-holes of her outer hull as she settled on an even keel and shook herself free from the sea. She had been to the very portals of Neptune's kingdom. She had dared the ancient sea king in his own domain, and she had returned from her venture the richer for her experience.

Reacting instinctively to the agonizing tension they had endured for the last ten minutes the men lining the rails of the escort tug let out a ragged cheer.

Hamilton swung himself through the narrow hatchway in the watertight bulkhead and ducked into the cramped confines of the bow torpedo room.

"I want to go through the checking routine on No 5 and No 6 tubes," he informed Martindale curtly.

The sub-lieutenant nodded and crouched down behind the heavy steel doors of the lower pair of torpedo tubes. Reaching forward he turned the lever of the inspection tap to No 5 and was rewarded with a stream of water that soaked the front of his uniform trousers. Shutting it off quickly he leaned across to No 6 tube and pushed the horizontal lever to the left. Nothing emerged from the spout of the tap and, returning the lever to the "off" position, he glanced back over his shoulder at the skipper.

"You see, sir. She's as dry as a camel's chuff."

"Try the drain valve."

The drain valves were used to empty the tubes into the bilge by hand if the pumping machinery failed. Martindale bent forward again, grasped the brass valve control, and began turning it clockwise. Almost immediately a powerful jet of water shot from the orifice and his mouth gaped in horror.

"Christ!"

"Turn that bloody valve off!" Hamilton snapped.

Martindale obeyed. Dazed by the sudden rush of water, he was unable to think straight and his hands worked automatically. The jet of water slowly died away to a harmless trickle and then stopped. The sub-lieutenant's face was white as a sheet as he stood up.

"My God, sir," he whispered. "No 6 was flooded up all the time."

Hamilton nodded and then glanced up at the bow-cap operating lever of the recalcitrant torpedo tube. The lever was set in the "neutral" position. So was the lever on No 5.

"I'll tell you something else, Mr. Martindale," he said quietly. "Both bow caps are open as well. That's why the water came out of the drain valve under pressure. If I had allowed you to open the rear door of No 6 while we were at 200 feet nothing on earth could have saved us." He turned to the torpedo gunner's mate. "Open the isolating and control valves, Newton. Then put on telemotor power and close the bow doors." He turned back to the sub-lieutenant as Newton began opening the necessary valves. "When the bow caps are shut I want both tubes pumped clear. Give me a call when it's done. I intend to inspect those tubes personally."

*We, Fairchild & Chandler (Construction) Ltd., Clydebank, handed over Job 738, constructed by us for His Majesty's Navy, at three p.m. o'clock this 18th day of June, 1939 off Loch Long. For and on behalf of Fairchild & Chandler (Construction) Ltd. HENRY J. DUNCAN.*

*Job 738 has been received, without prejudice to outstanding liabilities, from Fairchild & Chandler (Construction) Ltd., Clydebank, this 18th day of June, 1939.*

Hamilton stared down at the insignificant-looking piece of paper lying in front of him on the wardroom table and unscrewed the cap of his fountain pen. At least he could now sign his name with a clear conscience. His inspection of the two torpedo tubes twenty minutes earlier had exposed the mystery of the submarine's trim. And he knew that *Rapier* would never let him down again of her own volition.

"All's well that ends well, eh Captain?" Duncan said with a thin smile as he reached for the traditional glass of whisky.

Hamilton grunted without committing himself. His fingers played idly with the cap of the pen as if he was undecided whether to accept the submarine on behalf of the admiralty.

"Of course I should have remembered to warn you that we always flood the tubes by opening the bow caps when we're testing them at the yard," Duncan admitted. "An oversight on my part, I'm afraid. But fortunately there's been no harm done. I hope it didn't worry you too much." Hamilton's expression revealed nothing and Duncan looked anxiously at the document which was still awaiting the lieutenant's signature.

Hamilton put the pen down on the table. "Mistakes are bound to happen, Mr. Duncan," he said mildly. "I suppose I am equally to blame for my ignorance of shipyard methods. In the navy we always flood the tubes by pumping water from an auxiliary ballast tank in order to maintain trim. It never occurred to me that your men would use the bow cap method. In fact, as you may recall, I was unaware initially whether my crew or your men had carried out the flooding order."

Duncan nodded sympathetically. Hamilton wasn't the first submarine skipper he'd met who had no idea of the civilian way of doing things. He swallowed his whisky and looked at the blank paper as if willing Hamilton to sign it and put him out of his misery.

"And again," Hamilton continued, "I should have realized that your men would be unfamiliar with the Royal Navy's regulations concerning the position of the bow-cap operating levers. Our torpedomen always leave them in either the 'open' or the 'shut' position— never in 'neutral.'" He smiled faintly, as if excusing his concerns for minor details. "It's a small point, I know, but as you have seen for yourself, it's a vital one."

"Quite so, quite so," Duncan agreed hastily. "I shall

make a point of reminding my men to follow service practice in future." His laugh sounded a little hollow. "Can't afford to make mistakes in our line of business, eh?"

Hamilton looked up sharply. His eyes were suddenly hard.

"I'm glad you agree, Mr. Duncan. Which brings me to the final matter." He felt in his pocket, pulled out an empty matchbox, slid the tray open, and tilted it upside down over the table. A tiny black flake, the size of a bruised fingernail, which in many ways it resembled, dropped out and fluttered on to the virgin whiteness of the Acceptance Note. "Take a good look at it."

Duncan peered at the miniscule object and frowned. "What the hell is it, Lieutenant?"

Picking it up between his finger and thumb Hamilton held it as delicately as a jeweler examining a rare diamond.

"*This,* Mr. Duncan, is all that stood between you and death an hour or so ago." He tossed it toward the shipyard boss. "Keep it as a souvenir. And every time you look at it just remind yourself that this one insignificant flake of paint could have cost the lives of forty men."

Duncan shifted uncomfortably in his seat. He stared down at the black sliver like a man mesmerized by a venomous snake ready to strike. "I don't understand, Lieutenant."

Hamilton picked up his fountain pen again but he made no effort to sign the paper. He wanted Duncan to remember every word of the interview.

"I went down and personally inspected each torpedo tube once we'd surfaced and pumped them clear of water. I found that one of your laborers had slapped bituminous paint over the inside of the rear loading door to No 6 tube. And he'd let it run down so that it covered the small-bore feed pipe leading to the inspection cock. When Martindale turned the lever of the cock that flake of paint was blocking the outlet hole and, finding that no water was coming out of the inspection tap, he naturally concluded that the tube was dry.

"I was, of course, unaware of the cause of the trouble but I *did* know that we had perfect trim. And as that was impossible unless *both* lower tubes were flooded—your own figures proved that—I realized that something was wrong. That was why I refused permission when Martindale wanted to open up the tubes for inspection. Had I been as slap-dash as that painter in the shipyard we'd all be on the bottom of the Irish Sea right now."

Hamilton scrawled his signature on the paper, added his rank and status as commanding officer of *HMS Rapier*, and blotted the ink dry.

"There's your Acceptance Note, Mr. Duncan," he said coldly. "And thank God I won't have to trust *your* men to work on *my* submarine again."


# CHAPTER FIVE

In Hamilton's opinion, and despite everything the history books might say, war was infinitely more boring than peace. And as he had already endured six weeks of active service he felt more than qualified to pass judgement.

Huddled inside the warmth of his duffel coat and grasping his Ross binoculars with frozen fingers, he stared gloomily ahead as *Rapier*'s bows plunged into the black wind-torn sea and threw a curtain of stinging spray over the unsheltered bridge. The submarine rolled as the squall changed direction and he grabbed at a stanchion to maintain his balance. Looking over his shoulder he could see the two duty lookouts, Grainger and Harper, staring into the blackness and he wondered why the poor sods didn't admit they were wasting their time. Not even a trained eye could detect anything on a night like this.

How the hell they stood it was something he could never understand. In his own case it was the only way of life he had ever known. But Grainger had been working in the office of a city accountant less than two months earlier while Jimmy Harper, now looking like a bedraggled bat in his dripping oilskins, was pounding the stage of the Prince of Wales Theatre as a chorus boy. Either of them could have wangled a cushy job in the stores with the Brylcreem boys of the RAF—or, in Harper's case, found a place in an ENSA concert party. And yet here they were, facing the elements on a submarine, in the middle of the North Sea. Hamilton felt sure of one thing. When they'd joined the RNVR in 1937 they'd never thought of serving in submarines. And if they had, he concluded, they must be bloody fools.

He pulled the cover from the voicepipe and held his mouth close to the tube. "Engine room? Tell the chief I want to have a word with him." The ice-cold spray lashed his face with the relentless fury of monsoon rain and Hamilton dragged the hood of his duffel-coat over his head as he waited. "O'Brien? How much longer do you need the starboard engine for charging?"

"I can shut down the charge now if you want to, sir."

Hamilton ducked away from the voicepipe in search of shelter as a heavy sea swept over the foredeck casing, smashed against the steel ramparts of the con-ning-tower, and hurled a solid wall of black water over the bridge. He heard Harper being violently seasick as *Rapier* rolled wildly under the assault and he reflected dispassionately that the water streaming across the deck and gurgling noisily into the scuppers would save some unfortunate matelot the unenviable task of clear-ing up the mess later. Fighting his way back to the voicepipe he clung on tightly as the submarine crested a giant wave and crashed down into the trough that followed.

"I must have more power, Chief," he yelled into the speaking tube. "Connect up the starboard tail clutch and give me both engines. To hell with the charge."

With *Rapier* deep inside enemy waters Hamilton had no wish to get caught short of electrical power but, while the submarine remained on the surface, he *had* to have maximum revolutions from the diesel engines to hold the boat's head into the wind.

"Both propellors connected, sir."

"Well done, Chief. Full ahead both."

No submarine skipper in his right mind would have chosen to remain on the surface in a Force 9 gale but Hamilton was denied the luxury of an option. The next day's operational orders were due at midnight and *Rapier* could not submerge until the radio signals had been received. And there were still ten minutes to wait.

The extra power produced by the second diesel gave the submarine steerage way and Hamilton was able to hold the bows into wind to minimize the stomach-churning corkscrew motion. Not that it greatly improved conditions. *Rapier* still pitched steeply as the wave crests lifted her bows and she was rising and falling like a see-saw. It was no place for weak stomachs. The acrid tang of diesel oil interlaced with stale cabbage and the sour smell of vomit was, in itself, an unfailing recipe for nausea. And when allied to the motion of the boat the urge to be sick was irresistible. No one was immune and even Murray, the radio operator, had a bucket wedged alongside his table as he huddled miserably over the wireless apparatus waiting for *Rapier*'s call-sign from Northways—the block of flats at Swiss Cottage in North London where the flag officer (submarine) had his operational headquarters.

Like his German opposite number, *Kommodore* Karl Doenitz, Max Horton had a paternalistic affection for the men he commanded and, aware of his reputation, they in their turn respected him. Hamilton in normal circumstances would have cursed the man who was now forcing him to remain on the surface in this appalling weather just to receive a two-line wireless signal. And he would have added a few pithy comments about admirals sitting comfortably in overheated offices while he, and others like him, had to endure the wet and cold of a North Sea gale without respite night after night. But with Horton it was different. Twenty-five years earlier he had endured the same hardships when, as Britain's top submarine ace, he had scoured the frozen Baltic in search of enemy targets and as a veteran of underwater warfare he knew what it was all about. And so, like it or not, Hamilton ac-

81

cepted that *Rapier* had to remain on the surface and ride out the storm until the vital signal was received, decoded and acknowledged.

The voicepipe whistled shrilly and he flipped back the brass cover.

"Yes?"

"Control room, sir. Northways is transmitting. The pilot's decoding."

"All received, Number One. I'll be down. The quicker I see it the quicker we can get the hell out of this damned gale. Send the sub up to relieve me."

Gripping the edge of the conning-tower coaming, Hamilton braced his feet against the bucking motion of the deck while he waited the arrival of his relief. Twinkletoes, as Harper was known to his messmates, was no longer retching his heart up, having presumably got rid of the final remains of his supper, but his face was pale and drawn under the flapping brim of his sou'wester and it was clear that he, for one, wouldn't be sorry when they went to diving stations.

Martindale hauled himself awkwardly through the upper hatch, lurched hand-over-hand across the heaving deck and, clinging to the periscope standard for support, saluted his skipper.

"Reporting for duty, sir."

"Ready to take over the watch, Sub?"

Martindale was eager for his second stripe, and, after his error of judgement during the acceptance trials, he felt he had a lot of ground to make up if he was to get a promotion report.

"Yes, sir," he confirmed.

"Then you're a bigger damn fool than I took you for," Hamilton snapped. "You've been on deck precisely fifteen seconds. What do you think you've got—cat's eyes?"

Although the storm was easing as the wind veered to the south-west the submarine was still pitching sharply and Martindale swayed to maintain his balance. He accepted the rebuke in silence.

"Don't ever take over a watch until your eyes are completely adjusted to the darkness." Hamilton knew he'd been hard on the inexperienced junior and he tried to temper the sharpness of the rebuke with some friendly advice. "I know you were anxious to relieve me. And anyone who has stood watch for two hours in this sort of weather is keen to get below. But the safety of the ship is a hundred times more important than the comfort of one man or the eagerness of the other. The relieving officer should never formally take over until his eyes have adjusted to 100% night vision. That's the reason," he added, "why I change our lookouts at staggered intervals and not watch for watch. I know it's irregular but I don't give a damn about the regulations. I want to bring my boat back home at the end of a patrol."

"I think I can see okay now, sir."

"Good lad," Hamilton nodded encouragingly. "We should be diving in ten minutes or so. Stand by to clear the bridge as soon as you get the order."

The sweetly sour smell of fresh vomit rose up to meet the Lieutenant as he came down the conningtower ladder into the control room. After the biting coldness of the bridge the interior of the submarine was like an airless furnace and, despite his appreciation of the glowing warmth, Hamilton half regretted leaving the clean windswept chill on deck.

"Stand by for diving in ten minutes," he warned Collis as he dropped down from the ladder and pulled off his wet duffel coat. Taking care to avoid the slop bucket standing beside the chart table, he wedged his backside on the bottom rung of the ladder and began dragging off his sea boots. "How are the batteries?" he asked.

"95% full charge, sir. The chief seems happy with them."

Hamilton grunted. "If this bloody gale keeps us down for the rest of the night we're going to need every ounce of juice we've got to maintain our patrol routine. We're well inside the Bight and we daren't show ourselves until it gets dark tomorrow night."

"Couldn't we lie on the bottom with the motors off, sir?" Collis suggested.

"I'd like to, Number One. But my orders are to be in the vicinity of the Vyl lightship at midnight tomor-

83

row. There's no rest for the wicked when there's a war on."

Geoff Gilbert, *Rapier's* navigation officer, came through the access hatch of the bulkhead forming the forward defensive wall of the control room and handed a slip of paper to Hamilton. As the submarine's coding officer he was responsible for encyphering and decoding all radio messages. Hamilton took the signal flimsy and read it quickly.

SECRET. MOST IMMEDIATE.

FROM: FO(S)NORTHWAYS.

TO: CO RAPIER. REPEATED: STERLET, STYX, AIG 47, HQCC, OD.*

ORE CARRIER SOLDART LEFT BERGEN 18TH AM. TWO DESTROYERS REPORTED LEAVING WILHELMSHAVEN YESTERDAY (20TH) EVENING FOR ESCORT TO HAMBURG. SEEK FIND DESTROY. SUGGEST INTERCEPTION POSITION R. 0002N/I

"Acknowledge and give Northways our present position, Pilot," Hamilton instructed Gilbert. "Tell them will do."

He moved across the the chart table as the navigator made his way back to the radio compartment to encypher the reply. *Rapier's* midnight position was clearly marked on the chart. But, as Hamilton well knew, it was little more than an intelligent guess. The storm was still completely obscuring the sky and their last accurate fix had been obtained over eighteen hours earlier when Collis had caught a star sight just before dawn. Since then the submarine had been at the mercy of the swirling tides and currents of the German North Sea coast as well as the gale force winds sweeping down cross the Bight from Norway. The confidently pencilled cross on the map could, in fact, be anything up to

* The distribution of repeated signals was controlled by standard abbreviations. In this instance—Home Fleet, Admiralty, C-in-C Western Approaches, Admiral Commanding Orkneys and Shetlands, C-in-C Rosyth, Senior Officer Western Patrol (AIG 47); Headquarters RAF Coastal Command (HQCC); and Operations Division (OD).

20 miles from their true position. And it was nobody's fault.

Hamilton bent over the chart and pulled the angle-armed lamp closer as he studied the situation. Position R—a predetermined point set out in the Patrol Routine issued by flotilla before they left Rosyth seven days earlier—was just to the south of Sylt. Hamilton picked up the dividers and measured off the distance between their present estimated position and the suggested point of interception. Forty miles. He considered the problem. Assuming the two destroyers had left Wilhelmshaven around dusk, and assuming they were making thirty knots, and assuming they held a course which kept them inside the protection of their minefields, they could pass through position R an hour or so before dawn.

There were too many assumptions for Hamilton's liking but it was the best he could do. Northways' signal had been equally vague. And he must allow for the worst possible combination of circumstances if he was to ensure that *Rapier* was in the correct position for interception before the enemy ships actually appeared.

"Can we make it in time?" Collis asked anxiously.

"I shall want to know the reason why if we don't," Hamilton told him. "But it will mean running on the surface for the rest of the night." He reached for the voicepipe to the bridge. "Martindale? What's the weather like?"

"Improving slowly, sir. The gale has veered south and blown itself out. And the sea conditions are moderating. It even seems a good bit warmer, thank the Lord."

You'll learn, thought Hamilton. A rise in temperature was the last thing he wanted. Once the wind died away the warm front would bring mists and fogs in its trail and he needed good visibility to fix his position and find his target.

"Diving stations are cancelled," he told the sub. "We'll run north on the surface to make up time. And keep your eyes skinned. We've got a couple of Hun destroyers in the area."

Replacing the flexible speaking tube on its hook

85

above the plotting table Hamilton stared thoughtfully at the chart.

If his assumptions were right *Rapier* would be in position at least thirty minutes before the destroyers appeared. And if he was wrong about the enemy's speed they might have a tedious wait of anything up to four hours. In many ways he hoped he *was* wrong. A night torpedo attack had little to recommend it and he preferred to stalk his victims in daylight. But, again, if the fog came down as he feared, conditions would be equally difficult after dawn. Not that he was pessimistic about the operation. With three submarines spread thinly across the possible tracks of the destroyers they stood a fair chance of getting one of them. And as *Rapier* had pole position closest to the coast, Hamilton felt the odds were in his favor to make the interception. At least, he consoled himself, they were in no danger of being spotted by enemy aircraft if the threatened fog developed. So perhaps he should be thankful for small mercies.

He summarized the situation to Gilbert as soon as the navigator returned from the radio room and the two men bent over the chart to work out their best course.

"I reckon they'll come west through the Amrum Gap once they've cleared their minefields," Hamilton surmised. "They'll want to keep well outside the Danish three-mile limit."

"It's a possibilty, sir." Gilbert obviously wasn't so sure. "Personally I'd have expected them to keep inside Denmark's territorial waters to avoid our submarine patrols."

"You might be right, Pilot. I agree that's the route they'll take on their way *back* to Hamburg. But they won't want to risk being spotted by coast-watchers on the outward run." Hamilton paused and looked at the chart again as he weighed up the situation. He tapped his teeth with his pencil. "No—I'll stick to my hunch. Lay off a course for the Amrum Gap with an ETA of 4 am, Geoff. We'll dive when we get there."

"It's a hell of a gamble, sir," Gilbert objected. "We haven't had an accurate fix for nearly twenty-four hours. I don't want *Rapier* to end up on a mudbank off the Danish coast."

"I'll take full responsibility, Pilot. Lay off a course from our DR position at midnight. I'll do the rest." Leaving the navigator to work on the problem he walked over to Collis. "You'd better take over the rest of the watch from young Martindale, Number One. He's too inexperienced for this sort of caper."

"Aye, aye, sir."

"The pilot will give you a new course in a few minutes and I'll come up to relieve you at eight bells. We'll close up for action at the end of the morning watch." Hamilton yawned suddenly. He'd been on the go for twelve hours and he'd forgotten how tired he was. "I'm going to have a bite to eat," he told Collis and yawned again. "Then I'll have a quick kip. Call me immediately if anything happens."

On his way down the corridor to the wardroom Hamilton paused outside the submarine's miniscule galley. Poking his head inside he saw Rivenham busy over the electric stove.

"Where's the regular cook?" he asked.

Leading Seaman Rivenham grinned. "Down in the fore-ends mess with stomach cramps, sir." He grinned. "Must have been something he ate, sir. The Cox'n told me to stand in for him."

Hamilton looked doubtful. To the best of his knowledge Riverham was a Seaman Rating with no training whatsoever in the culinary arts. "What's for dinner?" he asked.

"Scrambled eggs, sir. Be dished up in a jiffy."

Hamilton nodded, pushed the curtain aside, and went into the wardroom. He threw his cap onto the armchair and settled himself expectantly at the table. Apart from a bully beef sandwich he hadn't eaten for eight hours and, with suitable reservations, he was looking forward to a hot meal. "Tinker" Bell, the able seaman who acted as *Rapier*'s wardroom steward, placed the plate in front of his commanding officer. Hamilton looked down at his dinner.

"What the devil is *that,* Bell?"

"Cook says it's scrambled eggs, sir." He lowered his

voice confidentially. "To be honest, sir, it looks more like . . ."

"I'd rather not have your colorful but no doubt apt description, thank you, Bell," Hamilton told him. The revolting yellow mess on his plate was nauseous enough without the added spice of Bell's lurid imagination. "Tell the cook I wish to see him."

"Sir!"

Bell vanished behind the curtained screen. Moments later he reappeared with an uncomfortable-looking Leading Seaman Rivenham. Both men stood to attention.

"What," asked Hamilton, prodding the jaundiced mess with his fork, "is this supposed to be, Rivenham?"

"Scrambled eggs, sir—like I told you in the galley, sir."

"And what culinary devices did you utilize in creating this masterpiece?"

"Beg pardon, sir?"

"How the hell did you cook it, Rivenham?"

"Well, sir, I boiled up the eggs to get 'em hard. And then I put 'em through the mincer. Seemed the most sensible way of doing it," he added by way of afterthought.

Hamilton struggled to keep his face straight.

"I'm sure you were doing your best," he said with a sigh. "Now get this stuff in the garbage. I'll make do with a sandwich and a mug of hot soup."

"Sir."

Rivenham picked up the plate with the expression of a man who had been terribly wronged and disappeared toward the galley to prepare the captain's sandwich.

"Some mothers do 'ave 'em, sir," Bell commented laconically as Rivenham departed. Hamilton allowed himself to smile. He nodded.

"They certainly do," he agreed. "Perhaps he was just trying to keep me hungry so that I'll hunt better when the time comes."

"Captain to the control room!"

The last echoes of eight bells had scarcely faded as the first lieutenant's voice crackled through the grille of the loudspeaker directly above the pillow of Hamilton's bunk. He was wide awake in an instant and had swung his legs over the edge almost before his eyes opened. Grabbing a grubby woollen sweater, he dragged it over his head and pulled on his sea boots.

"Four o'clock, sir," Martindale announced cheerfully as the skipper came through the hatchway into the control room.

"Where are we?" Hamilton asked Gilbert.

The navigator shrugged. "I wish I knew, sir." He bent over the chart and drew a large circle with his pencil. "Anywhere in this area. Your guess is as good as mine."

Hamilton nodded, grabbed the steel ladder, and swung himself into the lower conning-tower. Looking upwards toward the top hatch he could see the swirling dampness curling into the wet gray sky like tobacco smoke. He thrust his head through the upper hatchway and heaved himself onto the bridge. The warm front he had predicted earlier had brought thick fog in its wake and he could scarcely see across to the far side of the narrow bridge.

"Just our bloody luck, sir," Collis greeted him gloomily.

Hamilton made no reply. He stood with his hands resting on the rails staring into the fog and sniffing the damp air like a dog catching the scent of its prey.

"Stop engines!"

Collis centered the telegraph and the repeater bell tinkled far below in the bowels of the engine-room. A strange stillness descended over the bridge as the insistent throb of the diesels died away and the only audible sound was the gentle slap of the swell against *Rapier*'s hull plating. Hamilton stood with his head cocked to one side, listening.

"Can you hear anything, Number One?"

Collis instinctively held his breath as he listened. He could just discern a faint rustling, whispering from the fog somewhere ahead of the bows.

"Sounds like the waves breaking on the shore," he suggested diffidently. Hamilton nodded. He moved to the voicepipe with surprising speed.

89

"Clutches out! Switches on! Group down—half astern both."

The mudbank was probably no more than a hundred yards ahead—an invisible trap for the unwary in the all-enveloping fog. And with *Rapier* drifting slowly forward on the flood tide a valuable half minute had to be sacrificed while he changed over to the electric motors.* But Hamilton had no alternative. His hands gripped the rail tensely as he waited an eternity of seconds for the submarine to respond.

"Motors grouped down, sir. Half astern both."

*Rapier* slowly lost way as the propellers churned the muddy shoal water. A faint ripple drifted toward the bows from astern and, answering to the reversed thrust of the screws, she began to glide backwards. Hamilton waited for a few moments.

"Stop motors!" The submarine continued to drift astern with dead propellors as her skippers weighed up the situation. *Rapier* was clearly well to the east of her DR position and, utterly lost, they had got themselves tangled up in the maze of tiny islands and sandbanks fringing the North Sea coastline of Germany and Southern Denmark. If they continued to run northwards as originally intended they stood a bloody good chance of ramming the island of Sylt which was lying hidden in the murk only a few miles ahead.

The barometer was falling again and the hint of a breeze promised to clear the swirling mists within an hour or so of dawn. He walked across to Collis who was standing in front of the gyro repeater. Like his skipper, the first lieutenant found himself completely disoriented by the wall of fog which surrounded them on all sides.

"We'll have to chance our arm and steer by the compass, Number One. If we go westwards we should run clear of the shoals and find deep water. Then when the fog disperses later on we'll be able to take a fix and get back on station again."

* The diesel engines of a submarine cannot be put into reverse due to the clutch arrangement required for charging the batteries. If the vessel needs to be maneuvered astern it is necessary to switch over to the electric motors.

Collis nodded. Without an accurate fix there seemed no alternative although, like Hamilton, he did not relish the idea of striking blindly to the west and taking a chance. He felt it was his duty to voice the obvious objection. "If we happen to be *west* and not east of our DR position we might stray into *Sterlet*'s billet. They won't be expecting to meet a friendly submarine and they could mistake us for a U-boat."

"It's a chance we'll have to take," Hamilton conceded. The danger of mistaken identity had already crossed his mind. "But if we run submerged it's a thousand-to-one shot against them making contact. And if they do we may be able to signal to them on the Fessendon."* He turned to Thaker who was steering the submarine from the helm position on the bridge. "Alter course to 2-7-0."

"2-7-0, sir."

"Half ahead both."

The foredeck of the submarine was completely shrouded in a blanket of impenetrable fog and the stay-wires, glistening with drops of heavy moisture, vanished into the swirling dampness like the unsupported ends of an Indian fakir's rope. It was impossible to see the bows and Hamilton had to rely on the swinging needle of the magnetic compass to confirm *Rapier*'s sharp turn toward the west. For a brief moment he wondered whether he had done the right thing. But whether he had or hadn't, it was too late to worry.

"Control room reports Asdic contact, sir!"

"All hands clear the bridge. Stand by diving stations!" Hamilton hurried to the voicepipe. "Captain here."

Martindale sounded excited. "Asdic contact, sir. Positive. Approximately one mile on port bow."

"Tell Glover to hang on to it. And give him some back-up support from the hydrophones. Are we on lower steering?"

"Yes, sir."

"Depth reading?"

"Ten fathoms, sir, and deepening."

_____

* Underwater communications system.

91

Hamilton glanced quickly around the bridge to ensure that everyone was safely below.

"Steer 8 points to port. Full ahead both motors. *Dive—dive—dive.*"

"Group up—full ahead both! Open main vents. Hard a-dive!"

Hamilton swung his legs into the opened hatch as *Rapier*'s bows slanted beneath the surface. It was an eerie sensation. He could hear the water roaring into the ballast tanks and he could feel the deck tilt as the hydroplanes drove the submarine under the sea but he could see nothing and *Rapier* seemed to be sinking gently into the bottomless swirling fog. Pulling the hatch lid shut he pushed the clips home and inserted the pins. Then, climbing down through the darkness of the lower conning-tower compartment, he descended to the bright warmth of the control room.

"Level at thirty feet," he ordered as he reached the bottom of the ladder. Able Seaman Warren reached up to secure the lower hatch.

"Lower hatch shut and clipped, sir."

"Any further reports, Number One?"

"Yes, sir. Baker's located them on the hydrophones."

Hamilton nodded. "Keep her at periscope depth, Number One. I know we can't see a damned thing in this bloody fog but you never know your luck." He reached for the microphone of the loudspeaker system. "Close up attack team. I repeat. Close up attack team. Stand by torpedo room. Bring all tubes to the ready." Hamilton replaced the microphone, checked the gyro repeater, glanced up at the large dials of the two depth gauges, ran a quick eye over the glowing lights of the venting and blowing panel and, satisfied, went aft to the Asdic and hydrophone operators.

"What's the HE?" he asked Baker. Like many old hands in the trade, Hamilton did not altogether trust the Asdic equipment and he preferred the evidence of the human ear despite the electronic trickery that boosted the faint underwater sounds a hundredfold. The hydrophone operator scanned the range with his big circular tuner and, keeping one muffled headphone pressed firmly against his left ear, he leaned back slightly.

"Definitely two ships, sir."

"Merchant ships?"

"Could be. They're turbine powered. They seem to be running in some sort of formation—probably line ahead judging by the intensity variation."

"How about trawlers?" Hamilton acted the role of Devil's Advocate with conviction. He *had* to be sure. And by suggesting alternatives he was guarding against the hydrophone operator's natural inclination to regard every sound as a potential target. "*They'd* run in formation."

"Not at twenty knots, sir."

Hamilton looked thoughtful. Had *Rapier,* by the blindest stroke of luck, stumbled across the track of the two destroyers? He shrugged. Well, even in submarine warfare, coincidences were not impossible. Thank the Lord he'd dived as soon as he'd received the initial Asdic report. He turned to Glover.

"Does your box of tricks confirm the HE?"

Glover accepted the implied snub with good grace. He knew his apparatus was immeasurably superior to the hydrophones. Science allowed no scope for human error or wishful thinking. In all probability submarine skippers would be equally sceptical of the new radio-location sets when they were fitted.

"Speed confirmed, sir. My reading is actually 19 knots. I have echoes from two objects one cable apart.* Course approximately NNW with a range of one mile."

"Do you think they are trawlers, Glover?"

The Asdic operator did not intend to get drawn into a question of opinions. His job was to provide the skipper with solid accurate scientific fact.

"Sorry, sir. I couldn't say. The echoes only give me range, speed and course of target. I'd only be guessing."

The expression on Hamilton's face reflected his obvious disdain. The Asdic report was fine, but it didn't tell him the one vital fact he needed. What sort of vessels

* 1 cable = 100 fathoms = 200 yards.

were reflecting the echoes? He returned to the reassuring humanity of the hydrophones.

"What do you make of it, Baker?"

"Well, the HE's too heavy for trawlers. I'd say something more the size of a sloop or a destroyer. Definitely too light for a cruiser. I'd estimate a similar course and range to the Asdic report."

Hamilton nodded. "Thank you, Baker. Keep tracking and let me know as soon as they alter course or speed." He ducked back into the control-room. The attack team were closed up and, for a fleeting moment, he was reminded of the scene inside *Surge* on that fateful day Cavendish had taken her into Kiel Bay. He scribbled the hydrophone and Asdic reports in the rough log and turned his attention to the chart again. He still had no clear idea of the submarine's position but, provided they remained in deep water, it no longer mattered. Both targets were within torpedo range and the only factor of importance now was the position of *Rapier* relative to her intended victims. Bending over the chart he ruled a straight line running NNW and, after glancing up at the gyro repeater, ruled another line to represent the submarine's track one mile to the left of the other.

"Steer 0-0-5."

Finnegan, the helmsman, moved the wheel and as the gyro came onto 005 he brought it back into the midship's position. "0-0-5, sir."

"Up periscope!"

Hamilton peered intently through the eye-pieces as the top lens broke the surface. The fog was still with them but it was less dense and beginning to move as a rising breeze stiffened from the north-east. Visibility had improved to 100 yards—still hopelessly inadequate but the combination of the early morning sun and the freshening wind held a promise of better conditions in the near future. It was now solely a question of keeping *Rapier* within striking distance of the destroyers until the fog had lifted sufficiently to make a visual attack.

"Down periscope." Hamilton found it difficult to conceal his disappointment as he turned away from the 'scope. The next ten minutes would be crucial. With their superior speed the destroyers would be pulling away out of torpedo range with every passing second. If only this bloody fog would lift.

"HE slowing, sir. Estimated speed 10 knots."

"Are they altering course, Baker?"

"No, sir. Maintaining course on NNW."

Hamilton felt the adrenalin in his blood stream. *They still had a chance.*

"Up periscope!"

Even in those few short minutes the rising wind had started to clear the fog in earnest and visibility had now increased to half a mile. And, occasionally, where the warmth of the sun had scythed a swathe of clear air through the thinning banks of mist, considerably more.

A vague shape drifted ghost-like through the dampness on the very edge of visibility and Hamilton gripped the steering handles of the periscope more firmly as he strained his eyes into the murk. He wondered whether he dared to take a chance before he had positively identified his target.

"Start the attack! Target speed 10 knots—bearing *that!*" Yarrow, the electrical artificer, read off the calibration and passed it back to Gilbert at the fruit-machine. "Range . . . *that!*" The navigator moved the levers of the torpedo director to assimilate the data.

"Are the tubes flooded up?"

"Yes, sir."

"Open bow caps!"

The two fleeting shadows were a little clearer and Hamilton could identify them as slim, two-funnelled warships, with the low silhouette and long forecastle of destroyers. Yet there was something about their appearance that raised a doubt in his mind. Hamilton paused. He thought for a moment and dismissed the doubt. They were too far committed to the attack to change their minds now. And in any case, despite the reduction in speed, both targets were slowly moving out of range. Bending his eyes to the periscope he called off a fresh range and bearing and heard the whirring click of the fruit-machine digesting the information as Gilbert fed in the new data.

Suddenly and without warning the shadowy shapes of the targets vanished into a wall of dense fog and Hamilton lost sight of them. Keeping his fingers crossed he held the periscope lens on the same bearing and a moment later the two ships reappeared.

This time there could be no mistake. They were warships. But, with the benefit of improved visibility, Hamilton could see that despite their twin funnels and rakish lines they were not *Möwe* class torpedo boats. The smokestacks were too thin and they looked strangely old-fashioned in appearance.

"Stand by for salvo firing at one second intervals. Depth setting ten feet."

Three more minutes and they'd be out of torpedo range. Why the hell couldn't the damned fog clear for just a few seconds? He stepped back from the main periscope and moved into position behind the small attack periscope at the rear of the control room.

"Put me on director angle."

Gilbert passed the required figure to Yarrow. Reaching over the skipper's shoulders the artificer placed his hands over Hamilton's and guided the periscope to the calibration mark computed by the fruit-machine.

"On director angle, sir."

"Up periscope!"

The slender stalk of the attack 'scope rose up, cut through the waves with a minimum of tell-tale spray, and stared at the targets.

"Torpedo room—prepare to fire."

Hamilton could see only the blankness of an empty sea and his stomach knotted with tension as he waited for the two destroyers to move across the lens into the graticule sight. A shaft of bright sunlight suddenly gleamed on the surface of the sea and, for the first time since the attack started, Hamilton found himself with almost perfect visibility. He could feel the palms of his hands sweating as he clung to the periscope controls and waited.

The bows of the leading destroyer glided silently into the eye-piece, moving slowly from left to right as she steamed unwittingly across *Rapier*'s converging track. Hamilton watched her slide past and decided to concentrate on the second of the two ships. The destroyer following astern was a good five hundred yards closer than its running mate and the shorter range would improve the chances of a successful attack. Hamilton was not a greedy man. One in the bag would be quite enough. And he saw no reason for not selecting the easier target.

The leading destroyer had passed almost completely across the lens and Hamilton could see the build-up of wash along her beam as the stern came into view. He stiffened suddenly.

"Cancel attack! Check! Check! Check!"

Collis looked up sharply. Something had obviously gone wrong. He waited for the follow-up orders for a change of speed and course. The tables must have been turned and they had become the hunted and not the hunters. But why the hell wasn't the skipper taking evasive action? Similar thoughts were chasing through the minds of the submarine's two coxswains, Ernie Blood and Bill Tropp, but they remained stolidly imperturbable at the controls of the hydroplanes with the disciplined resignation of experienced veterans. Whatever might be happening topsides the skipper knew best.

"Down periscope!"

Hamilton's face was still pale with tension but he showed no signs of urgency as he stepped back from the 'scope. Reaching up he pulled down the microphone of the submarine's tannoy system.

"This is the captain. The attack was abortive. Let's hope we have better luck next time. All hands stand down to patrol routine." He replaced the microphone. "Maintain depth and course. Reduce to half ahead both."

He glanced quickly around the control room. In the anticlimactic aftermath of an abortive attack it was easy to lose concentration and make a mistake. He checked the dials and warning lights one by one. Everything was fine. He had a good team.

"I didn't think we ought to start another war just yet," he said enigmatically to no one in particular. "And, in any event, I reckon we ought to beat Hitler before we do."

It was Collis who asked the question trembling on the lips of every man in the control room.

"What happened, sir?"

Hamilton shrugged and scratched the lobe of his left ear. "Nothing much, Number One. We've spent the last few hours chasing a couple of Danish torpedo boats. Fortunately the fog lifted just in time for me to recognize their ensigns and identify them. So much for all these scientific boxes of tricks they give us. You can't beat your own eyes when the cards are down."

"Nearly another Copenhagen, sir," Collis observed drily.

Hamilton grinned at the irony of the situation. "You know, Number One," he said slowly. "Until you mentioned it the thought hadn't even crossed my mind."

# CHAPTER SIX

The night express from Perth to London had never been Hamilton's favorite means to travel. And the difficulties of war had done nothing to improve its attractions. Even the cramped interior of *Rapier*'s wardroom was comfortable compared with the overcrowded railway carriages of the train now rattling and wheezing its weary way into Crewe Junction three hours behind schedule.

It was Hamilton's first taste of life ashore in wartime Britain. And he had already decided it was an experience he could have well done without. He rubbed a clear patch in the steamy condensation on the window and stared out into the blackout. Not a glimmer of light was visible in the darkness and it was difficult to imagine that he was passing through the heart of industrial England as the train clattered its way through the night.

There were only two first class coaches and both had been reserved for the brass-hats—admirals who had not been to sea in the last ten years and red-faced army staff officers who spent their allotted five-hour working day sitting peacefully behind empty desks at the War Office. What space remained in the cosseted warmth of the sleeping compartments was taken up by sleek civil servants with brief cases, bowler hats and neatly furled umbrellas.

The rest of the passengers—and that included everyone from the rank of major or lieutenant commander down to the lowliest matelot and scruffiest private soldier—were cramped into the crowded and unheated third class carriages where they had to share the rigors of wartime travel with a mixture of civilians also on their way south. The narrow corridors were blocked by enormous green canvas kitbags, officers' suitcases, civilian luggage, and the snoring bodies of those unable to find room in the seating compartments. It was impossible to walk the length of the coach to reach the toilets and, even if anyone had succeeded in doing so, their urgent journey would have proved so much wasted time. The senior non-commissioned officers of all three services, with a cunning learned from long experience, had commandeered the cabinet-sized compartments for their own private accommodation and, propped comfortably against the lavatories and washbasins, they slept peacefully with the satisfied air of pampered guests in a four-star hotel.

The restaurant car was packed with humanity but totally devoid of food while a fault in the train's hot water system meant that even the British serviceman's traditional cup of tea was not available. Seated at the bare wooden tables the soldiers played cards, told jokes, or sang obscene barrack-room songs. The lack of facilities and home comforts did not worry them. Life on the Perth Express was no worse than living under canvas in hastily erected camps. And there was the added advantage that the sergeant-major was safely imprisoned in a lavatory at least three coaches away in the rear of the train.

Hamilton himself was wedged uncomfortably into a corner. A private from the Pioneer Corps was sitting opposite him playing unrecognizable but irritatingly mournful tunes on a battered mouth-organ while an over-large flight-sergeant, smelling strongly of beer and hair oil, rested his head on Hamilton's shoulder and snored defiantly in his ear. Rank carried no privilege on the night express. It was a case of every man for himself. And every woman—if you could find one!

Having completed three patrols *Rapier* had gone into Rosyth dockyard for a routine overhaul. But whatever hopes Hamilton may have entertained for a brief spell of leave had been quickly dashed by an urgent signal from London instructing him to attend an admiralty conference. There had been no time for anything.

Dalrymple, the flotilla commander, gave him an important-looking sealed envelope which was to be delivered to the flag officer (submarines) personally; the paymaster handed him a railway warrant; and Bell, *Rapier*'s wardroom steward and unofficial captain's servant, carried his suitcase to the station. And now, as the express crawled into Platform 9 at Crewe, Hamilton located his case under a pile of kitbags and fought his way to the door in the hope of stretching his legs for a few minutes before continuing his journey.

But despite its grandiloquent title the Perth–London Night Express was going no further. An engine breakdown on a north-bound train had disrupted the schedule and, after a hasty consultation in the stationmaster's office, the officials of the London Midland & Scottish Railway had decided to turn the London Express around so that the stranded passengers from the north-bound train could continue their journey to Glasgow. The fact that they were leaving themselves with another trainload of travelers in exchange did not, apparently, enter into their calculations.

Hamilton stumbled his way across the blacked-out station, found the RTO's office, and demanded to know what was going on. The harassed army lieutenant shrugged helplessly.

"God knows, old boy," he admitted. "There's a troop train coming down from Liverpool in half an hour but I gather it won't be stopping. And they're holding the line clear for a munitions train after that." He ruffled through the melange of dog-eared papers on his desk. "You might be able to get the Birkenhead Mail at 5:35 on Platform 8 if you're lucky," he suggested helpfully.

Hamilton could see the milling throng of expectant passengers on the opposite platform and decided that "luck" was an understatement.

"Now see here, Lieutenant," he said in his best quarterdeck manner. "I'm due at the admiralty for an important operational conference by noon tomorrow. Surely you can pull a few strings and fix me up."

The RTO seemed singularly unimpressed. He jerked his thumb in the direction of three red-tabbed staff officers waiting patiently on a hard wooden bench. "If I can't do anything for *them,* old boy, I certainly can't do anything for *you.* Now be a good chap—go and get yourself a cup of tea and stop bothering me. I've got a job to do. Don't you navy wallahs know there's a war on?"

Hamilton turned away angrily and started walking down the platform toward the buffet. A large propaganda poster glared down at him—its message spelled out in bright red letters twelve inches high—*IS YOUR JOURNEY REALLY NECESSARY?* The corners of his mouth turned down sardonically. Is it hell!

"Hi there, Nick! It *is* Nick Hamilton, isn't it?"

The total unexpectedness of hearing a woman's voice calling his name in the middle of Crewe Station brought him to an abrupt halt. As he turned he saw the trim figure of a second officer in the Wrens. Her face looked vaguely familiar but somehow he couldn't quite place it. He hesitated.

Suddenly the cogs of his memory clicked. Good God Almighty! It was hardly surprising he hadn't recognized her immediately. The last time he'd seen Caroline she had been lying stiff-nippled, wide-legged, and naked on a rumpled bed. She looked somehow different in uniform.

"Well I'll be damned—Caroline!" It was an ungallant greeting but she could understand his surprise. "What the hell are you doing here?"

"Waiting for a train like you." She stepped forward and kissed him lightly on his cheek. "Darling Nick. It's been months. I haven't heard a word from you since we were at Gerry's place in August." She pouted. "I thought you'd forgotten all about me."

"As if I could," Hamilton lied. "But this is my first spell ashore since the war started. Any news of Gerry?" he asked in a transparent attempt to change the subject.

"Haven't you heard?"

"No," Hamilton said shaking his head. "I've been too bloody busy driving my submarine around the North Sea to read the gossip columns. What's the silly bastard done now?"

"He's dead."

They had been walking slowly down the platform.

101

Now Hamilton stopped in his tracks. He turned and looked at Caroline in disbelief.

"Gerry is dead! He can't be . . . what happened?"

"I don't know all the details," she explained. "He was driving his new Maserati in Sicily the week war broke out. Apparently he skidded out of control, hit a wall, and the car burst into flames. It was on an isolated bit of road miles from anywhere. By the time the ambulance arrived it was too late."

"But there was nothing about it in the newspapers," Hamilton protested. "I couldn't have missed seeing it."

Caroline's normal flippancy was subdued. She nodded understandingly. In her own way she liked Hamilton. And the memory of their weekend in Norfolk had remained fresh in her mind. To be truthful she was looking forward to a repeat performance.

"I suppose there was so much war news that week it got pushed out," she said. "I did hear a rumor that they'd put a D-notice on the story but I don't see why they should have done. Gerry wasn't a secret weapon or anything."

Hamilton took her gently by the arm. He found it difficult to believe that Cavendish was dead. It seemed impossible. "Come on. Let's find this damned buffet place and drown our sorrows in a cup of tea." They made their way down the platform in silence and, as they approached the carefully screened entrance to the station buffet, he asked casually, "How did you find out about it if it wasn't in the papers? I didn't know there was anything going between you two."

"Oh, Mummy's in Monte Carlo for the winter. She saw it in a French paper and wrote to me."

Hamilton steered the girl through the doors of the refreshment room, found her a table heaped with dirty crockery and discarded cigarette ends, and made his way through the crowds to the counter. He was glad of the opportunity to hide his inner feelings. There might be a war on, but apparently one section of British society could still afford its winter holidays on the Riviera.

"Yes, love?"

The woman behind the counter reflected the general filth of the noisy overcrowded buffet. She had a cheap headscarf tied over her bleached hair and her once

102

white overall was now a dirty shade of gray splashed with the brown stains of spilt tea. Her fingernails were indescribable.

"Two teas, miss." Hamilton decided he didn't fancy eating any food which might have come into contact with her hands.

She slopped dark brown liquid from an ancient copper urn into a pair of chipped cups, dashed a minute quantity of milk into the brew, and banged them down on the counter.

"Sorry, love, no sugar. That'll be fourpence." She leered at him with a gruesome imitation of a Betty Grable smile and Hamilton hurriedly slapped four copper coins on top of the wet counter.

"It doesn't look very appetizing," he warned Caroline as he joined her at the table. "But it's wet and warm." He sipped it cautiously and grimaced with disgust. "Any ideas on how I'm going to get to town by twelve o'clock?"

Caroline drank a mouthful of tea and replaced the chipped cup on the table with the same polite delicacy she would have displayed drinking from Royal Worcester china in the drawing-room.

"No problem, darling," she said coolly. "I'm escorting Vice-Admiral Weatherly and he's got a reserved compartment on the Birkenhead Mail. I'll sweet-talk him into letting you join us."

Hamilton had seen Weatherly from a distance before. And that was the way he preferred to see him. The former chief-of-staff had a reputation that even a concentration camp commandant would have envied. The thought of anyone sweet-talking "Tug" Weatherly into anything, especially a mere chit of a girl young enough to be his granddaughter, was an intriguing thought.

"Okay," he said easily. "See what you can do. Just for old time's sake," he added with a touch of diplomacy.

"On condition you do *me* a favor, darling."

"Of course."

"I'm going on leave as soon as I've delivered the old gas-bag to the admiralty. I'll be staying at the Strand. If you can get away from your silly old conference why don't you come over and make a night of it?"

Hamilton was not accustomed to girls who issued open invitations. But the memory of that weekend in Norfolk was still fresh in his mind. And after fourteen weeks without a woman he was not inclined to pass up the opportunity when it was offered.

"Lieutenant Hamilton, officer in command of *Rapier*, sir."

Rear Admiral Mabberly nodded as Grenson brought Hamilton into the conference room and introduced him.

"Glad you could make it, Hamilton. Take a seat. I'm standing in for flag officer (submarines). He's been called to a special meeting with the PM and the War Cabinet. Damned nuisance but we'll have to manage as best we can."

No one had given Hamilton the slightest indication of what the conference was about and, on entering the room, he was surprised to find he was the most junior officer present.

"This is Grenson, captain (S) at Harwich," Mabberly rumbled on. "He'll be your new chief. We want you to bring *Rapier* down from Rosyth to join the 16th Flotilla as soon as the refit is completed. That's why we had to call this meeting in such a hurry."

It seemed a little unnecessary to arrange a conference just because he was being transferred to a new flotilla and Hamilton wondered warily what it was all leading up to.

"You'll have heard about this damned U-boat operating off the East Coast," the rear admiral growled suddenly. "Playing hell with our inshore convoys."

"No, sir," Hamilton said, shaking his head. "I've carried out three war patrols in the last fourteen weeks. To be honest I haven't had time to even keep up with all the news from my own operational area let alone elsewhere."

Mabberly grunted. "Put him in the picture then, Grenson," he told the officer sitting at his side. Pulling a pipe from his pocket he rammed it into his mouth and wriggled deeper into his armchair while captain (S) took over.

"We've had a U-boat working off the East Coast

104

covering roughly an area stretching from Clacton to the Wash," Grenson explained briefly. Picking up a pointer he indicated the location on the wall chart behind the admiral's chair. "It could be more than one boat but from the evidence available I doubt it. This U-boat skipper knows his stuff. He hides up somewhere in the shoal waters along the coast and then pounces on our convoys as they run south. By the time the escorts have located him he's scuttled back behind the sandbanks and hidden himself again."

"Couldn't we locate him from the air, sir?" Hamilton asked.

"It's been tried, Lieutenant. But, firstly, we don't have enough aircraft to spare for long duration searches—the best the RAF can do is a couple of Ansons—and, secondly, the enemy apparently knows of a deep water channel of which even the official hydrographer is ignorant. At any rate it's not marked on our charts."

Hamilton passed no comment. He did not really understand what all this had to do with him. If they were sending *Rapier* down to join in the search it seemed a waste of time to call a special conference for a routine flotilla operation. And why weren't the other submarine commanders present?

"What d'you think, Lieutenant?" Mabberly barked through the smokescreen of his pipe.

"I really don't know, sir. As Captain Grenson has pointed out, it would seem that the U-boat captain knows something we don't." Hamilton could not resist the opportunity of a sly dig at the Establishment. "The man you needed for this problem was Lieutenant Commander Cavendish. He knew the inshore waters of that area better than anyone. But, of course, he's dead now."

"How did you know about that, Lieutenant?"

The question came from a commander sitting on his own in a discreet corner of the room. He had not been introduced with the others and Hamilton looked at him with open curiosity. Rear Admiral Mabberly hurriedly repaired the omission.

"This is Commander Mason. He's on the staff of the

105

DNI* and has been invited to attend the conference as an observer."

Hamilton nodded his thanks to Mabberly. He met the commander's eyes coolly. "Actually, sir," he explained, "I read about it in a French motoring magazine." He paused deliberately. "I was rather surprised to find no mention of it in our own newspapers."

"We have been unable to obtain official confirmation of Cavendish's death," Mason told him. The tone of his voice was flat and disinterested. "In the circumstances higher authority decided to issue a D-notice on the story until we know for certain. What do you know about it? You were one of his friends, weren't you?" The commander worked a sarcastic inflexion into the last question and Hamilton flushed.

"I know nothing beyond the press report, sir. And, with respect, Gerry Cavendish was a very good friend of mine."

"Glad to hear it, Lieutenant," Mabberly interjected with bluff heartiness. "A first-rate officer. A bit wild, mind you, but none the worse for that. I knew his father well." He sucked on his pipe. "That's the reason I asked you to attend this conference," he explained. "I knew you used to do a spot of sailing with young Cavendish along this particular section of the East Coast. Thought you might have picked up some local knowledge from him that could help us out with our problem."

Mabberly was one of the old-school. Straightforward and decent. But Hamilton knew he was lying. They hadn't brought a staff officer down from the DNI just for the fun of it. And with characteristic stubbornness he ignored the rear admiral's attempt to pour oil on troubled waters.

"But as Cavendish is no longer an officer of the Royal Navy," he asked Mason pointedly, "why issue a D-notice?"

The commander shrugged. "As I explained—it was put out by higher authority. The admiralty had no hand in it. I can only assume they wanted to avoid any complications over his estate until it was officially con-

* The Director of Naval Intelligence.

firmed. After all, Cavendish was a wealthy young man. It could be extremely embarrassing to distribute his assets and then discover that he is still alive."

"*Is* he still alive, sir?"

Mason's eyes hardened to ice. He had no intention of becoming involved in an argument with a junior submarine commander and he was annoyed by the rear-admiral's failure to call Hamilton to order. "It is not my business to say whether he is alive or not, Lieutenant. You must draw your own conclusions. I am merely pointing out that until his death is official there are many good reasons for keeping it quiet." He turned to Mabberly impatiently. "Can we not get back to the subject of our discussion, sir?"

The rear-admiral nodded approvingly. "I agree, Commander. I think we *have* rather strayed from the point." He peered across at Hamilton from under his fiercely bushy eyebrows. "Well, Lieutenant? Do you feel your special knowledge of the East Coast is sufficient to help us trap this damned U-boat?"

"I'm doubtful, sir. As I have already pointed out Cavendish was the expert." He saw Mason raise his eyes to the ceiling with mock impatience. "But I'm willing to do my best."

"Excellent—excellent. I've had to bring you down from Rosyth because *Rapier* is the only small submarine available for the moment. Most of our U-class boats are patroling the German coast in the hope of intercepting *Graf Spee* or *Koenig* on their way home from the Atlantic."

The two pocket-battleships had been causing great concern at the admiralty. The threat which they posed by their presence on the Atlantic trade routes and by their tip-and-run raids on single merchant ships had become a top priority. The most recent intelligence reports placed *Graf Spee* safely in the Indian Ocean where she was likely to cause less harm but, for the moment at least, *Koenig* had vanished. It was suspected that *Kapitan* Mikel was returning to Germany via the Denmark Straits and, in the hope of ambushing the raider on the last stages of its homeward run to the Fatherland, all available British submarines had been dispatched to intercept and torpedo the 10,000 ton pocket-battleship.

"Speaking in confidence, gentlemen," Mason was unable to conceal the complacency in his smile," I think I can promise you that neither of these raiders will get back to Germany. *Graf Spee* has already rounded the Cape and Commodore Harwood's squadron should make contact within the next seventy-two hours. As for *Koenig*, she will never escape the submarine trap we have set up across the approaches to Germany's main naval bases."

"I hope your intelligence proves more reliable than the report *Rapier* was given about those two German destroyers a month or so ago," Hamilton said sourly. "If the fog hadn't lifted at the last moment I'd have bagged a couple of Danish warships. And that *would* have put the cat amongst the pigeons!"

"That particular intelligence came via Section VI," Mason snapped curtly. Hamilton was beginning to irritate him and he intended to slap him down once and for all. "I understand that the War Cabinet has the greatest faith in their informant. If I have my facts correct the two German destroyers sailed precisely in accordance with the reports passed to the DNI by Section VI. Any difficulties that may have occurred were due to the unfortunate fact that *your* submarine was more than thirty miles off course."

Mabberly's fierce glance warned Hamilton to remain silent. He wanted to tell the pompous staff officer that in the weather conditions prevailing at the time *Rapier* was bloody lucky not to have been a *hundred* and thirty miles off course. But he bit back his retort and contented himself with an angry scowl. Nevertheless he was intrigued by Mason's reply. He wondered why Section VI—the special intelligence unit directly responsible to the War Cabinet—should be so certain of their source of information.

"How soon can you get your boat down to Harwich, Lieutenant?" Mabberly asked. He wanted to bring the conference to an end before Mason and Hamilton came to blows. And he wondered why the DNI's department had insisted on engineering this particular meeting. Obviously they wanted to find out something about Hamilton. So far as Mabberly could see he seemed decent enough. But, of course, he had no background. That was the trouble with these men promoted from the lower deck—you never really knew who they were or where they came from.

"Provided the dockyard has completed its work I could bring her down in a couple of days, sir. Say Tuesday by the very latest."

Mabberly raised a quizzical eyebrow at Grenson. "Will that fit in with your plans, Captain?"

"Yes, sir," Grenson confirmed. "Things have been fairly quiet for the last week or so. I reckon the U-boat has returned to base for refueling and fresh torpedoes. If my staff reports are accurate I would anticipate the enemy to be back around the middle of next week."

"Good—then that's settled." Mabberly turned to Hamilton. "You can leave for Rosyth first thing tomorrow. I'll lay on an aircraft for you from Northolt." Hamilton nodded his appreciation. That meant he'd be able to spend the night with Caroline. Mabberly stood up and held out his hand. "Good luck, Lieutenant. I want this damned U-boat run to ground. And I'm relying on *Rapier*."

Hamilton shook the rear admiral's hand, stepped back two paces, replaced his cap, and saluted.

Mabberly watched him leave and waited for the door to click shut. Then, raising his bushy eyebrows, he turned to the commander.

"Well?" he asked. "Do you think he knows anything?"

Mason shrugged. "I wouldn't like to commit myself at this stage, sir. But we'll soon find out."

The December sun was fading gently behind Admiralty Arch as Hamilton passed through the sandbagged entrance, exchanged salutes with the sentry, and stepped out into Trafalgar Square. Glancing up at the gray wintry sky he saw the silver barrage balloons hanging in the air like a shoal of bloated fish and he wondered when, if ever, the war was going to start in earnest. Despite numerous false alarms London had not received a single bomb and there seemed to be some sort of gentlemen's agreement between the politicians on both sides not to launch air attacks on each other—probably because it would place their own precious lives at risk.

The American press was calling it the "phony war" and Hamilton had to agree that there was more than an element of truth in the gibe. Admittedly the RAF was flying night raids over Germany but they were dropping nothing more lethal than propaganda leaflets. And even if the pen *was* mightier than the sword he could see little likelihood of winning the war that way. Only the Royal Navy, it seemed, was involved in any real fighting, but even the war at sea amounted to little more than sporadic air raids and furtive submarine attacks. Yet the price was already painfully high—the battleship *Royal Oak* sunk by a U-boat in the safety of the main fleet anchorage at Scapa Flow and the giant aircraft carrier *Courageous* snapped up by another enemy submarine while on anti-U-boat patrol in the Channel. A ludicrous example of the misuse of air power by men who did not understand modern warfare.

Still immersed in his thoughts, Hamilton crossed the lower part of the Square and made his way past Charing Cross station into the Strand. Khaki and RAF blue seemed the predominant colors among the busy crowds and he felt faintly conspicuous in his dark blue naval uniform as he pushed his way through the homegoing travelers thronging into the station. Crossing the road he turned up into Covent Garden and, walking eastwards, began thinking about the conference he had just left. It had been an odd sort of affair—almost as if they wanted to discover something about him rather than about Cavendish. He wondered what the hell was going on. And why all this mystery about poor old Gerry. Either he was dead as the French newspaper had reported or he was still alive. And if he *was*, what did it matter to Naval Intelligence or anyone else beyond his family and his immediate friends? He could understand why they wanted to check the facts. It could be embarrassing if they distributed his estate and he then turned up alive and kicking. But that was a matter for his solicitors, not the DNI. And, just supposing he *was* still alive, where the hell was he?

The public houses bordering the fruit market were

open—the Covent Garden area enjoyed liberal licensing hours—and, turning out of Russell Street into Bow Street, he decided to call at the *Globe* for a quick stiffener before going on to see Caroline. The coldbloodedness of her casual proposition was a little unnerving and he felt in need of some Dutch courage.

Pushing open the heavy wooden doors he wriggled through the blackout curtains and entered the crowded bar. It was already dusk outside and the bright lights were blinding to eyes accustomed to peering into the blackness of the North Sea. There did not seem to be a bare inch of drinking space left and the babble of noise was more deafening than standing in the center of *Rapier*'s engine room when the diesel units were running full blast. Pushing his way to the bar, he caught the eye of the blonde barmaid and ordered a gin and tonic.

The girl smiled cheerfully, thrust the glass under the measuring optic of an upended bottle of Booth's Finest Dry, and winked at Hamilton's reflection in the long painted mirror behind the bar counter. She pushed up against the valve lever to make it a double, flicked open a small bottle of tonic water with an expert twist of the wrist, and put the glass down on the counter in front of him.

"That'll be two bob, love," she told him. "And seeing the navy's done it again you can have half of it on me."

Hamilton didn't argue. Even with his submariner's allowance a lieutenant's pay was barely adequate to live on—22/6 a day didn't go far in wartime England. And he had a feeling that Caroline was going to be expensive. She was certain to demand dinner as a *quid pro quo* for her services. Or perhaps he had got her wrong. She might be one of those girls who did it for King and country. Reaching into his pocket he found a florin and gave it to the barmaid.

"Why? What's the navy done now?" he asked.

She rang up the price of the drink and dropped the coin into the drawer.

"Didn't you hear the news on the wireless?"

Hamilton shook his head. "No—I've been in conference most of the afternoon. What's happened?"

The girl put her elbows on the counter and leaned forward. She made sure that Hamilton could see down the front of her low cut blouse. "The navy's been knocking hell out of the *Graf Spee*. According to the last bit I heard the Germans have taken shelter in some place—Monte Verdi or something like that."

Hamilton recalled Mason's remarks about the South Atlantic and he focused a mental picture of the map in his mind.

"Montevideo?" he suggested.

"That's the place, sailor." She winked again. "Ever been there? They say join the navy and see the world, don't they?"

"That's what they say," Hamilton agreed. "But I wouldn't believe it if I were you." It was certainly shattering news and he wondered what the full story was. If Commodore Harwood had tackled the pocket-battleship's six powerful 11″ guns with only his three underarmed cruisers he'd certainly got guts. They didn't stand a chance on paper. He put his glass down. "Any news of the *Koenig?*" he asked.

Rita's blank expression indicated that she didn't know what he was talking about.

"The other raider," Hamilton explained. "*Graf Spee* was working the South Atlantic shipping routes and the *Koenig* was operating further north."

The barmaid shook her head. "No—they never mentioned anything about the other one." She looked at him quizzically. "Why? Do you want them to save that one for you?" she asked.

Hamilton grinned. "If you can arrange it, yes please."

"Sorry, sailor. Even *I* couldn't manage that." She leaned forward across the bar again so that the front of her blouse gaped invitingly. Hamilton had seen it all already. But he wasn't averse to a second showing. "I could manage to save *something* for you," she offered. "We shut up shop at 11:30."

"And that's when you open for business?"

Rita smiled. "No—that's when I'm free."

Hamilton finished his drink. He put the glass back on the counter. "Well," he grinned. "If England expects, I guess I'll have to come around at 11:30 and do my duty." He pushed the sling of his canvas gas-mask case over his right shoulder. "See you later, England."

England gave a little shiver of anticipation as she watched him go out. Then demurely tightening the front of her blouse she advanced imperiously on two impatiently thirsty army officers at the other end of the bar.

As Hamilton walked down toward Wellington Corner he had to remind himself, not for the first time in his life, that he was an officer and a gentleman. Somehow he could never understand why the two things went together. Why the hell should a gentleman be an officer? Or, for that matter, an officer a gentleman. And from what he had seen and heard since he had been commissioned Hamilton was not altogether sure that he really wanted to be either.

He didn't fit in and that was all there was to it. Not that his brother officers treated him differently to anyone else in the wardroom. But in some subtle way he was always aware that he was not one of them, not one of the exclusive club that made up the commissioned ranks of the Royal Navy in 1939. He couldn't ride to hounds. And he didn't shoot. He was an outsider and he knew it.

Hamilton had never had anyone question his authority. On board ship where discipline was paramount and everyone was equal in the face of God and the sea he was accepted for what he was—an officer of His Majesty's Navy. There was no room for class distinction in a warship cleared for action or a submarine stalking its target unseen beneath the waves. That was when Hamilton enjoyed his status for what it was. At times like that a man had only to be a good officer and, provided he was fair and honest with the men who served him, whether he was a gentleman or not counted for nothing. But off-duty, on leave, or doing the social rounds, it was a different matter.

The older officers were, perhaps, a shade more tolerant. They'd been through the rough-and-tumble of shipboard life and they took a man for what he was. But the younger officers, his contemporaries in the

113

service, led a gay dilettante existence that bored him silly by its shallowness and lack of purpose. And the women who fluttered around them were, if it was possible, even worse. Hamilton was no prude but their brittle life-style and unending demands for childishly selfish excitement, sexual or otherwise, somehow filled him with disgust.

He turned into Aldwych and made his way slowly toward the hotel. That was all that silly bitch Caroline really wanted—a lover who could satisfy her. And, when he had done so, she would get bored with the game and turn to someone else. He paused in the shadow of Bush House and stared up at the night sky. Perhaps one day the war would start in earnest and, when it did, he wondered how the Bright Young Things would react to the bombs, the blood, the crashing buildings, and the screams of the dying. It might bring them to their senses and turn them into useful citizens. He doubted it but he was prepared to be open-minded.

Pushing his way through the swing doors of the Strand Hotel he found a uniformed commissionaire in the vestibule. He was wearing the crowned stripes of a sergeant-major and it was easy to see that he knew what it was all about.

"Which is Second Officer Faversham's room?"

The watery eyes of the commissionaire stared at him for a moment as if weighing up whether Hamilton was everything his two gold rings proclaimed him to be. Ex-warrant officers had an uncanny knack of spotting the outsider. *And* cutting him down to size.

"Is the lady expecting you, sir?"

Hamilton, too, had learned by experience. He ignored the question. Instead he put his hand in his pocket and slipped a pound note into the discreetly ready palm. The commissionaire winked.

"Better go up the back stairs, sir," he whispered hoarsely. "The management don't usually like ladies entertaining in their rooms. Second floor—Number 3."

Hamilton realized he had passed the test. It was surprising what a tip could do. With a pound in his pocket he could pass muster for a gentleman with any commissionaire in London. He nodded distantly and started up the stairs . . .

Caroline looked fluffily pert without her uniform. She obviously did not believe in wasting valuable time. The bed was turned back in readiness and the transparency of her nightdress did nothing to conceal the whiteness of her slender body.

"I thought about having dinner first, Nicky darling," she told him as he came into the room. "But we can always go out for a bite afterwards."

Hamilton did not tell her there wasn't going to be any afterwards. He had already made up his mind to show the silly bitch that he'd only accepted her invitation for one reason. And when he'd had what he wanted he intended to go. She'd probably accuse him of being no gentleman. And she'd be right. He wasn't.

He had taken her with cold efficiency, bringing her to a screaming pitch of excitement that wailed through the thin walls of the hotel room. And as she lay sprawled on the bed afterwards she looked like a fragile china doll that had been thrown across the nursery floor by a petulant child. He should have felt sorry for her. But he didn't. And as he began pulling on his clothes he could see a film of tears misting her eyes.

Caroline had served her purpose. She had found him a comfortable seat for the remainder of his journey from Crewe to London and she'd had her reward. He reflected cynically that it was probably the only useful thing she'd ever done in her shallow wasted life.

Bending over the rumpled bed he kissed her gently on the lips. She grasped his hand and pressed it against the firmness of her naked breasts.

"Don't go, Nick. Stay with me. Love me again."

Hamilton withdrew his hand before the sensual contact of the swelling nipple had time to reawaken the urges in his body.

"Sorry," he lied. "I'm due back at the admiralty for another damned conference in half an hour. I'd love to stay with you but . . ." He left the promise of the sentence unfinished and Caroline inelegantly sniffed back her tears. Then, picking up his greatcoat, he opened the door and stepped out into the hotel corridor with-

115

out looking back. Caroline watched the door close behind him and buried her face in the pillow.

The silken warmth of Caroline's room and the dank chill of the air-raid shelter were worlds apart. Yet they were both in the same city. The bare concrete walls were moist with damp and the air smelled of wet cement and fresh, dug earth. A piercing draught whined through a gap in the tarpaulins that screened the narrow entrance and Hamilton shivered in the darkness of the vault.

The girl stirred contentedly as he lit two cigarettes from the same match and passed one to her. She was snugly naked beneath the warmth of his dark blue greatcoat and it fell away to her waist to expose the fullness of her heavy breasts as she moved. Wrinkling like walnuts in the sudden chill the thrusting nipples hardened eagerly as he reached toward her.

Looking down at her Hamilton wondered why he had wasted his time with Caroline. Rita had everything the pampered Caroline lacked—warmth, earthy excitement, and the undemanding gentleness of a woman who understood the love a man needed. She had been waiting for him outside the entrance to the *Globe* as promised. And with no possibility of finding a hotel room at that time of night they had slipped unnoticed into the air-raid shelter which had been conveniently erected on the corner of Russell Street.

Rita handed Hamilton her half-smoked cigarette as she sat up. "I suppose I'd better get dressed," she said casually. "If I miss my last bus home the old man'll lock me out."

He watched as she bent forward to put on her brassiere and he wondered whether it was just one of the many chance encounters that happened between men and women when a country was at war.

"I've got to get back to my ship tomorrow," he explained as she began to fasten the front of her blouse. "But I'll come and find you next time I'm in London."

Rita laughed to hide her embarrassment. "That's what they all say," she told him teasingly. "Ships that pass in the night."

"I'm serious," Hamilton protested. Digging into his

pocket he pulled out a small oblong card. "You can always contact me at that address. And I'll give you a ring as soon as I get back."

Rita tucked the card into her handbag, swung her legs off the wooden bunk, and stood up to straighten her skirt. "We'll see," she said. She wanted to believe him but commonsense warned her not to be silly. Officers in the Royal Navy were not usually interested in barmaids, decorative or otherwise. By tomorrow he'd have forgotten all about her. A strange tension had developed between them and she giggled suddenly to break it. "If I *do* see you again I hope you won't make me work so hard next time."

Hamilton's flush was mercifully hidden by the darkness. Perhaps he *had* been a trifle too optimistic in meeting Rita only ten minutes after leaving Caroline. But when you were young the possibility of failure rarely crossed your mind. He promised himself he would not make the same mistake again.

They emerged from the shelter like two children escaping from the kitchen after raiding the larder, exchanged self-conscious grins with the policeman standing on the corner, and walked toward Aldwych hand in hand.

"I catch my bus here," she told him as they reached the tailend of a queue. "It's starting to rain. You'd better get along."

Hamilton hesitated but he could see she wanted him to go. Leaning forward he kissed her lightly on the cheek.

"Goodnight, sailor," she whispered. "And thanks for everything."

"Goodnight, England. I'll come and call for you as soon as I can get another 48-hour pass."

The No 15 bus squealed to a stop at the head of the queue, the waiting passengers moved forward, the conductor rang the bell, and she was gone. Hamilton stood on the edge of the pavement and watched the red double-decker vanish out of sight into the blackout.

The rain was falling more heavily now and, turning up his collar and pushing his hands deep into his greatcoat pockets, he started walking toward Trafalgar Square.

# CHAPTER SEVEN

"Convoy now moving north-east under cover of smoke. Torpedoed collier is fine on our starboard bow—range about two miles. On fire and sinking."

"Poor bastards," Bill Tropp grunted as he jockeyed the angle of the bow hydroplanes to maintain *Rapier* at periscope depth.

"They'll be okay," Hamilton said reassuringly. "They've got a couple of boats launched and sea conditions are good."

Geoff Gilbert leaned over his charts to mark off the approximate position of the doomed ship. "I make them about five miles from the coast, sir."

"Thanks, pilot." Hamilton swung the periscope onto a fresh bearing. "Fortunately they're not our problem. Our job is to find the U-boat that did it."

Grenson's prediction to Rear Admiral Mabberly had proved uncannily accurate. Having joined the 16th Flotilla a day earlier than anticipated *Rapier* had left Parkstone Quay on the flood tide the following morning and picked up Convoy MK-43 off the SW Shipwash buoy as it headed toward Barrow Deep *en route* for Tilbury and London.

The operational orders issued by captain (S) were characteristically clear and unambiguous. *Rapier* was to remain on the surface in the middle of the convoy until such time as a U-boat attack developed. She was to then dive immediately and steer a westerly course toward the coast to prevent the enemy submarine reaching its favorite hiding place amongst the shoals. *Rapier*'s position in the center of the convoy would, Grenson hoped, conceal her presence from the U-boat's hydrophones. The clattering engine noises created by the merchant ships and their escorts would effectively mask the throbbing beat of the submarine's diesels.

The convoy itself was to reverse course under cover of smoke as soon as the U-boat attacked. And, with brutal frankness, Grenson instructed the convoy commodore to abandon any torpedoed ships and leave survivors to fend for themselves.

Captain Nicholson, commanding the convoy escorts, was given similar orders. His ships were to take up a line to the east of the Sunk LV and, dividing into two separate groups, they were to search down the Knock Deep and Kent Deep respectively. With a British submarine operating below the surface in close proximity to the convoy all forms of depth charge attack were strictly forbidden and Grenson's intention was to use the escorts as a defensive outer ring to force the besieged U-boat inshore.

The plan was simple. And it was foolproof. The ring was to be cleared of all ships, leaving the two submarines to fight a duel to the death. In Hamilton's opinion, however, there was one flaw in Grenson's elaborate scheme. Everything depended on the U-boat captain playing the game by the same set of rules. And from what he had heard of the enemy skipper, *Rapier*'s commander thought such a probability highly unlikely.

"Any HE?"

Leading Seaman Baker shook his head. "Not a peep, sir." Bending over his apparatus he twiddled the ranging knob and stepped up the volume of his amplified receiver.

"Search inshore," Hamilton instructed. He turned to Gilbert. "Can you give me a fix, Geoff?"

The navigator glanced at the chronometer over the chart table, made a rapid calculation, and drew a line on the map subtending at 90° from their diving position in the center of the convoy. He marked a cross and ringed it.

"Take over periscope watch, Number One."

Hamilton joined the navigator at the chart-table. In his mind's eye he translated the surface situation he had seen through the periscope onto the map and, taking a pencil, he quickly sketched the approximate position and courses of the convoy and the escort forces.

The merchantmen were steaming hard for the Outer Gabbard lightship—the rendezvous point laid down in Grenson's orders—while Captain Nicholson's destroyers and armed trawlers, already split into two groups, were moving south toward Long Sand. All that remained in the immediate vicinity of the submarine was the unfortunate *Marshbank* with her stern sticking up forlornly from the gray sea and the two lifeboats pulling for the shore which was just visible through the mists five miles to the west.

Hamilton stared down at the chart and tried to put himself in the place of the enemy commander. Where the hell could he hide while he waited for the hue and cry to die down? Any attempt to escape eastwards into the empty wastes of the North Sea was impossible while the escorts ranged up and down the distant horizon and, knowing the German Navy's healthy respect for British Asdic, Hamilton thought it unlikely that he'd even try.

He could, of course, move northwards. But that would bring the U-boat too close to the approaches to Harwich. As an intelligent man he would know that the Harwich destroyers would join the hunt with minimum delay and it would be foolish to steer a course leading directly across their path. In addition a northerly course would put the U-boat within range of the new-fangled radio-location masts at Felixstowe and, while Hamilton knew little of their top secret functions, he had little doubt that the *Kriegsmarine* was equally cognizant of their existence.

So if the U-boat commander wanted to escape from Grenson's carefully laid trap he *had* to head inshore toward Stone Banks and then creep slowly down the coast in the general direction of the shoals and sandbanks off Foulness. And providing the enemy could hold off his pursuers until nightfall he would have a good chance of making a high-speed escape on the surface when darkness descended.

Hamilton turned away from the chart.

"Steer 2-4-0."

"2-4-0, sir!"

"Still no HE, Baker?"

"Nothing positive, sir. I've got faint noises on bearing 3-5-0 at maximum range. But it's the wrong effect for a submarine."

Hamilton scratched his ear. The sounds Baker was picking up were almost certainly the Harwich destroyers racing out to join the hunt.

120

"Only seven fathoms, sir," Gilbert warned as he watched the trace from the needle of the echo sounder.

Hamilton took one final look at the chart. "Can you see the NE Gunfleet buoy, Number One?"

"Yes, sir. Bearing fine on the port bow—range 1500 yards."

"HE bearing 2-3-0, sir," Baker broke in excitedly. "Electric motors—speed about five knots."

Hamilton mentally congratulated himself on correctly estimating the enemy's intentions. But, if Collis had the NE Gunfleet buoy in sight, the U-boat must be steering straight for disaster on the shoals of West Rocks. A glance at the chart, however, quickly deflated his optimism. The last hydrophone report placed the German vessel slightly south and west of *Rapier*'s mean course and that meant she would probably avoid the mudbanks by a hairsbreadth and find the deeper waters of Goldmer Gat. Obviously *Herr U-boat Kapitan* knew the area like the back of his hand. Or else he was plain bloody lucky!

Hamilton had always regarded Cavendish as the supreme expert on the problems of inshore navigation along the East Coast. But his German opponent seemed to be equally knowledgeable. He wondered whether he and Cavendish had ever raced against the U-boat commander in pre-war days. German and Dutch yachtsmen often competed in the more important events and his deftly confident handling of the enemy submarine suggested first-hand experience of the hazards involved.

"Down periscope!" Collis got out the way smartly as Hamilton snapped the order. "Bring her up to 20 feet. Steer two points to port."

*Rapier* glided upwards and leveled off with the top of her conning-tower barely three feet below the surface.

"Full ahead both motors."

"Full ahead it is, sir."

The submarine surged forward under full power and Hamilton wondered what would happen if he miscalculated and ran them head-on into a sandbank. Outwardly calm he walked across the control room and stood behind Leading Seaman Baker.

"I think target has increased speed, sir," Baker told him.

So the U-boat commander was trying to maintain his lead. Obviously the *herr kapitan* was keeping hydrophone watch as well. He shrugged. Well, two could play at that game. If he could keep on the U-boat's tail there was a good chance of forcing it further inshore toward the treacherous mudbanks.

"Target altering course, sir," Baker reported from his listening post. "A two point turn to port as far as I can estimate."

Hamilton swore but maintained course and speed until *Rapier* reached the U-boat's turning position. His quiet command reflected none of the tension gripping his body.

"Two points to port, helmsman."

Geoff Gilbert noted the course change in the rough log and marked it off on the plot. Projecting their track forward he saw they were heading straight for Gunfleet Sands. He glanced at the echo sounder for confirmation.

"Five fathoms, sir. And shoaling."

"Up periscope." Hamilton ignored the timely warning. If the U-boat had enough water under her keel to get through there was no reason to suppose that *Rapier* was running into danger. But, all the same, it was worrying. They needed Gerry Cavendish in the control room on a job like this. If there *was* an uncharted deep-water channel somewhere ahead he would certainly have known about it.

The U-boat had vanished from sight and even the high magnification search lens was unable to locate the whisper of spray thrown up by the stalk of the enemy periscope. The flat unattractive coastline around Clacton was clearly visible through the heavy mist and, on the port side, a sharp chop on the sea indicated the sandbanks lurking just below the surface. It was a treacherous area for navigation and even the admiralty charts were ominously noted *Banks constantly changing*. Most sensible seamen kept well clear even in fair weather. Yet, despite the thickening mists and closing visibility, Hamilton knew he was allowing himself to be drawn deeper and deeper into the trap.

"Contact lost, sir! No HE audible."

"Stop motors!"

Collis passed the order back to O'Brien in the motor room and the vibration tingling the steel deck-plates under their feet faded away.

"Down periscope."

Hamilton rubbed his chin thoughtfully as the column hissed back into its well. The U-boat skipper had obviously killed his engines to prevent *Rapier*'s hydrophones picking up the telltale sounds. But, if the submarine had stopped, it was difficult to see what advantage he had obtained by the ruse. Hamilton walked back to the chart and stared down at the map. *Banks constantly changing.* Perhaps the Hun had managed to wriggle through one of the narrow channels and the sound of his engines was being masked by a convenient sandbank. In the circumstances it seemed the only plausible explanation.

*Rapier* drifted slowly in the 2 knot current as Hamilton reviewed his options. There seemed to be only one thing he could do.

"Group down. Slow ahead both motors." The soft hum of the motors vibrated through the hull again as the submarine moved slowly ahead. "Up periscope!"

Hamilton knew he was taking a gamble. He had no clear idea where the U-boat was lurking and the spray from *Rapier*'s periscope would betray her position to the waiting enemy as soon as it broke surface. If the U-boat had worked its way round to the east the British submarine would be a sitting target for a torpedo.

But nothing happened and the tension inside the control room gradually eased as *Rapier* pushed on. The scent might be cold but the hounds were still eager. Hamilton swung the lens to the south more in desperation than hope. Suddenly his hands tightened on the guide handles and his thumb flicked the high magnification search lens into position.

He peered through the eye-piece again. There could be no mistaking the thin plume of spray. But how the hell had the U-boat passed across the Gunfleet Sands without surfacing? The more Hamilton considered the conundrum the more incredible it appeared. The chart soundings showed only two feet of water and not even a surfaced submarine could pass through that depth without grounding. Yet somehow the U-boat had succeeded *while still submerged!*

"Periscope sighted moving due east—range 1000 yards."

"But that puts it the other side of Gunfleet Sands," Gilbert objected. "It can't be."

Hamilton was glad someone else shared his puzzlement, even though he was not prepared to admit his concern to the crew.

"Take a look for yourself, Pilot," he said stiffly.

"Sorry, sir. I wasn't meaning to doubt your word. It's just that I can't see how the hell it was done not unless they've started building U-boats with wheels on them."

Collis obviously did not share Geoff Gilbert's faith in the skipper. He turned away from the diving control panel.

"With respect, sir," he said quietly. "Perhaps I can take a look. Two heads can often be better than one at times like these."

Hamilton was not sure whether to be annoyed or not. He wondered whether Collis was casting doubt on his ability. But, on the other hand, the first officer was right. A double check would do no harm. He stepped back and gestured toward the periscope. "Be my guest, Number One. Bearing 1-7-0."

Collis grasped the handles and pushed his face into the rubber cups. Hamilton saw him swing on the bearing and hold the target in view. Then, quite deliberately, he turned the lens to starboard, stared intently through the eye-piece, and stepped back.

"You're quite right, sir," he admitted. "We're to the west of Gunfleet and the U-boat is the other side of the sands steering east."

Hamilton made a mental note that Collis had double-checked the submarine's position relative to the coast. And that smacked of insubordination. He let it pass for the moment. Ordering the periscope to be lowered he dropped into his tubular steel armchair to think the problem over in his mind. Casting back into his memory he tried to recall the method Cavendish

124

used to pick out the uncharted channels when they were racing. Something to do with seagulls. *Yes*—that was it. Gulls tended to dive for fish in the shallowest water. And Cavendish used to claim that the deep channels could always be picked out by steering for the strips of water separating the flocks of feeding birds. It had seemed a fanciful idea at the time and Hamilton was sure Gerry had been pulling his leg. And yet . . .

"Up periscope!"

Swinging the lens in the direction of Gunfleet Sands he watched the sea birds bobbing gently on the surface waiting for food. Every few seconds one of the gulls would thrust its head under the water and emerge triumphantly with a silver fish glinting in its beak.

"Steer two points to port. Stop motors."

His prime concern was to avoid scaring the birds away from their feeding-ground and he allowed *Rapier* to drift gently with the flood tide as he surveyed the surface of the sea. There was certainly a distinct gap between the two groups of birds and the water dividing them looked a shade darker. The U-boat had obviously crossed the sand bank somewhere close to that particular spot but with only the doubtful evidence of the seagulls to guide his decision Hamilton decided not to risk going through submerged. The enemy may have done so. But there was a limit to the chances one could take and get away with.

"Stand by to surface. Slow ahead both." Hamilton checked the situation once more. "Down periscope. Surface."

"Close main vents. Planes hard a'rise. Blow all tanks!"

*Rapier* rose smoothly through the final few feet. She emerged from the sea in a bubbling froth of water and the gulls screeched into the sky protesting shrilly at the sudden appearance of a stranger in their midst.

"Up periscope."

Hamilton only intended to remain surfaced long enough to clear the sandbank so there was no point in opening the hatches. "Two points to port . . . steady . . . midship's helm."

Finnegan swung the wheel and Hamilton prayed that he had guessed correctly as he saw the bows turn toward the darker water separating the two groups of feeding gulls. The submarine thrust its nose between the submerged mudbanks and eased gently through the invisible gap.

"Twenty feet, sir."

Gilbert sounded surprised. The charts showed less than one fathom—yet, miraculously, there was sufficient depth of water under the keel to slide the submarine through in a semi-submerged condition. No wonder they hadn't spotted the U-boat. The enemy commander must have trimmed his boat down and gone through the channel partially awash with just the upper section of his conning-tower showing above the surface.

"Ten feet, sir! Shelving rapidly!"

"Full ahead both!" Hamilton snapped. If they were going to run aground he wanted *Rapier* on full power to force her through the mud by sheer brute strength. It was obvious he'd misjudged the location of the channel slightly. "Left rudder, Finnegan . . . steady . . ."

*Rapier* lurched gently as her keel touched bottom but her propellers thrust the submarine forward against the mud and, as the bows found deep water again, she slid clear. Hamilton wiped the perspiration from his face. Peering into the eye-piece again he searched to the north-west just in time to see the stalk of the enemy's periscope sneak upwards for a quick observation before discreetly vanishing beneath the surface again. It was a fatal error on the part of the U-boat's skipper. And as he caught a fleeting glimpse of the questing periscope Hamilton was suddenly freed from the anxiety of an ambush. His prey had disclosed its secret hiding place. And he was the hunter once again.

By bringing *Rapier* to the surface to clear the mudbank Hamilton could now use the superior speed of the submarine's diesel engines to close the gap with the fleeing U-boat.

"Go over to main engines, Number One."

"Grouper down—switches off. Clutches in. Start main engines."

"Gun crew to close up!"

Hamilton doubted whether a surface duel would be necessary but he could not afford to take chances.

126

Once the enemy skipper realized his danger it was always possible he'd come up and fight it out at close quarters. And Hamilton had no intention of getting caught off guard against such a wily opponent. He continued to con *Rapier* through the periscope for the same reason even though the submarine was in surface trim. His ability to dive on the button could be a decisive advantage in an emergency.

"Enemy surfacing!"

The U-boat commander had finally woke up to the fact that his pursuer was closing the gap. And he obviously intended to adopt the same tactics—a flat-out attempt to get away by using his powerful diesel engines. For a brief moment Hamilton was reminded of the excitement he had experienced in his yacht races with Gerry Cavendish in these self-same waters. But now there was an important difference. This time he was not striving for a silver cup or a fancy medal. This time the victor would win the right to fight again and the loser would die.

"Enemy turning to starboard . . . one—two—three points. Now steady."

White spray spumed back from the sharp bows of the U-boat and black diesel smoke belched from the exhausts as the enemy submarine built up speed.

"Three points starboard!"

*Rapier* swung south as Hamilton gave chase. But with the U-boat now running pell-mell for East Barrow at nearly 17 knots her advantage in speed was quickly lengthening her lead.

"Target turning through eight points to point—running due west."

As the U-boat doubled back toward the coast Hamilton suddenly remembered the shallow channel intersecting Sunk Sands. According to the chart it had a maximum depth of 9 feet at the Winter Low Water Mark and, with the afternoon tide in flood, there was probably just sufficient water to squeeze through in surface trim. If he could steer *Rapier* safely through the narrow gap and cut off the corner he could intercept the U-boat before it reached deep water. It was a chance well worth taking. No 5 Barrow buoy was already on the submarine's starboard hand and he lined the bows up carefully with the bell-buoy on the other side of the sandbank in Black Deep.

"Steer 1-5-0! Torpedo room stand by!"

Hamilton flicked onto the high magnification lens and found his next two navigation marks—No 5 and No 6 buoys which lay beyond the sandbank in Black Deep. The U-boat was firmly committed to its course and there was little danger of it diverting from its arrow-straight track. If Hamilton's calculations were correct, he could, by taking the more northerly route, cut off his prey's retreat a few hundred yards short of the deep water channel. His thumb returned the periscope to normal power so that he had a panoramic view of the attack situation.


Pilot Officer Kerr was cruising quietly home having just completed the second operational mission of his brief career. And, flying at 5,000 feet, he could see the flat coastline twelve miles ahead as he followed Beresford's Blenheim across Long Sand. Circling aimlessly over the empty wastes of the North Sea had no place in Kerr's idea of aerial warfare and he still felt bitter about his appointment to Coastal Command. His tally of two operational patrols had done nothing to assuage his resentment and, as he guided *Yellow-4* toward the three tall towers of Clacton pier, he decided to make another application for a posting to Fighter Command the next time he saw the adjutant.

*Red Leader to Yellow-4. Red Leader to Yellow-4. Are you receiving me?*

Kerr lifted one hand from the control column and pressed the headset closer to his ears.

*Yellow-4 to Red Leader. I hear you loud and clear.*

*Do you see submarine at two o'clock?*

Kerr stared out through the perspex canopy and looked down at the rippled surface of the sea. He had never seen submarines on the surface before but he assumed Beresford was correct. Keeping his eyes on the two vessels carving white arrows through the gray water 5,000 feet below he reported back to his wing leader:

*Yes, Red Leader. I've got them. Over.*

Due to faulty staff work 89 Squadron had not been

advised of Grenson's plan. Falling within the command structure of 6 Group, they had no priority communications channel with the Senior Naval Officer at Harwich and it would be twenty-four hours before the squadron received details of the navy's anti-U-boat operation. They were, of course, aware of Convoy MK-43—information on merchant shipping movements came direct to the squadron from Coastal Command HQ—but the daily operational briefing from group had contained no mention of British submarines in the area.

Looking down from his position high in the sky Kerr could see the shallow water covering the sandbanks as clearly as they were shown on the charts. And he watched with idle interest as one of the two submarines headed toward a light green patch of sea. The significance of what was about to happen suddenly struck him and he pressed his radio button.

*Yellow-4 to Red Leader. That silly bugger's going to run himself aground at any moment. Over.*

*Don't get so excited Yellow-4. How much fuel do you have? Over.*

Kerr glanced down at his gauges. The needles were flickering into the final quadrant. But there were still two reserve tanks untouched.

*Yellow-4 to Red Leader. About 30 minutes. Over.*

Flight Lieutenant Beresford stared regretfully at the two submarines as he made his decision. It was difficult to believe that two U-boats would risk coming so close inshore. But, according to the morning's operational briefing, there were definitely no friendly submarines within 20 miles of the coast. Nevertheless it was a little odd. He pushed the microphone close to his mouth.

*Red Leader to Yellow-4. I'm nearly out of fuel so I'll have to miss the fun. Attack whichever target is easiest. But check identity. We don't want any mistakes. Good hunting, Bill. Over and out.*

Kerr banked to starboard and put *Yellow-4* into a gentle dive as Beresford continued on course toward the coast. For the moment he was too busy flying the aircraft to watch his potential targets and a gloved hand banged him on the shoulder as he leveled off at 2000 feet. Sergeant Dunne, the Blenheim's navigator, pushed his mouth close to the skipper's ear to make himself heard above the roar of the engines.

"You missed your vocation, sir. You should have been a bloody fortune-teller!"

Kerr looked out over the starboard wing and grinned as he saw what Dunne was getting at. The submarine he had reported to Beresford a few minutes earlier was now stuck high and dry on the partially submerged sandbank.

"Is it a U-boat, sir?"

Kerr shrugged. "No good asking me, Sergeant. All submarines look the same so far as I'm concerned." He pushed the control column forward. "Let's take a closer look."

As the bomber swept toward the stranded submarine Dunne's eyes searched anxiously for its companion. Suddenly he spotted a swirl of white water just over a mile to the east.

"The other boat's diving, sir."

"I'll have to let him go, Sergeant. We can only manage one at a time. And I'd rather concentrate on that bloody idiot sitting on top of the sandbank."

The Blenheim roared low over the bubbling circle of water which the second U-boat had left behind on the surface and then, skimming the wave-tips, headed toward its helpless comrade.

"What d'you think?" Kerr asked Dunne as they passed over the grounded submarine and began climbing away in a lazy circle. "Is it one of ours?"

"It's not flying the White Ensign if that's what you mean, sir." Dunne picked up his binoculars and examined the rust-streaked hull. "I can't see any identification marks at all."

Kerr took the Blenheim back to 2000 feet and circled cautiously. The stranded submarine resembled a dying whale washed ashore after a fierce storm. It looked neither British nor German. But, as he had told Dunne, all submarines looked the same to him. The sergeant was still studying the U-boat carefully through his glasses.

"They're opening the upper hatch, sir. Looks like they're making for their deck gun."

"That settles it, then," Kerr said decisively. "I'm not

getting myself shot up by some bloody Hun. Open the bomb doors and let's get cracking."

Dunne climbed out of his seat, wriggled forward under the pilot's position, and stretched full length on his stomach to peer through the bomb-aimer's window set in the floor of the aircraft's fuselage. His thumb jabbed the switch.

"Bomb doors open, sir."

Kerr gunned the engines to full power, tilted the Blenheim onto its port wing, and began diving toward his helpless target. It was the first time he'd attacked anything in cold blood and his hands trembled with nervous excitement as he leveled off for the final approach.

"ASI shows 220 knots, Sarge. Put me on target."

"You're too far over to the right, sir." The aircraft juddered as Kerr kicked the rudder. "Still too far . . . that's better . . . okay. Hold her on that, sir." Perspiration beaded Kerr's face and he felt slightly sick. He reached up and wiped the sweat away with a gloved hand. He wondered how long it would be before they heard the sullen crump of bursting flak and the anticipation did little to ease the butterflies in his stomach. What the hell was he supposed to do now?

"Get the nose down, sir!" Even Dunne's normally phlegmatic tones sounded excited as they crackled through the head-set. "We're overshooting."

Kerr eased the nose down a fraction and, in his anxiety not to over-run the target, throttled back to lose air-speed. It was a fatal mistake. The nose fell away with terrifying suddenness and, banging the throttles open, he pushed the stick forward to counteract the stall. He heard Dunne swear as they swept over the submarine and he cursed himself for his ham-fisted handling of the attack. Pulling the stick back he climbed for height. A sudden burst of machine-gun fire added to the tension and he turned around in his seat to see if they'd been hit.

"That'll take the edge off their appetites," he heard Mitchell chuckle over the intercom.

"Take it easy, sir. It's a piece of cake now," Dunne encouraged his skipper. He felt sorry for Kerr. Two weeks out of an Operational Training Unit and this

131

was only his second combat patrol. What a time to find a U-boat. "If you level out earlier on the next run you'll be okay, sir. But for God's sake don't alter speed. Just follow my instructions. And all you've got to do is keep her flying."

"Thanks, sergeant. Sorry for the cock-up. I'm getting the hang of it now, I think."

"I wish you two bastards would pull your fingers out!" Mitchell broke into the intercom. As the Blenheim's midships gunner he had little to do, so had taken over the duties of look-out. "The second U-boat's surfacing again. If you don't get your skates on we'll get caught in their cross-fire!"

The bomber banked sharply to starboard as Kerr opened the throttles and climbed for height. For God's sake! If he couldn't cope with one bloody U-boat how the hell was he going to manage two? Mitchell was right. They *had* to destroy the stranded submarine. And fast!

# CHAPTER EIGHT

The sudden lurch followed by the grinding rasp of shingle under the keel could mean only one thing and Hamilton responded to the emergency almost before it had happened.

"Hands to collision stations! Close all watertight doors! Stop engines!"

*Rapier*'s bows rode upwards like a tank bestriding a trench and, as the stern fell back, she came to rest at an angle of 20°. Pandemonium reigned for a few seconds as crockery, tools, stores and loose equipment cannoned wildly in all directions. The men, hurled to the deck by the impact, swore angrily as they climbed back on to their feet rubbing their bruises. But an oppressive silence soon followed in the wake of the unexpected disaster and, with the intuitive reaction of true submariners, the crew strained their ears for the sound of leaking plates and sniffed cautiously at the air for the first trace of chlorine gas.

"Could be worse," Collis observed dispassionately. "At least we've gone aground on the flood tide."

Gilbert checked his tide tables calmly. "High water's due in ninety minutes," he confirmed. "We should have another two feet of water by then, sir."

Hamilton nodded. Like Collis he felt no immediate alarm over their predicament. It was ironic that *Rapier* should have grounded in a channel which, according to the official admiralty chart, had more than sufficient depth for a safe passage while the U-boat, cutting across the sandbank by an uncharted route, should escape scot-free. He remembered laughing at a similar incident before the war when John Kimmins had grounded *L-86* on a sand-spit in Stokes Bay. But it wasn't so funny when it happened to you.

Satisfied that the submarine was in no immediate danger, and still furious that his prey had escaped, Hamilton went back to the periscope to survey the surface situation. Then, almost as an afterthought, he tilted the upper lens to carry out a routine sky search. He could see two Blenheims to the south-east but took little notice of them. The RAF had been informed of the U-boat hunt and he did not feel unduly worried by their presence on the scene. And, in any event, the two bombers were heading toward the coast and were obviously returning to base at the end of a North Sea patrol.

He closed up the handles of the periscope. Fortunately *Rapier* was stranded on soft ground and according to the reports coming back to the control room her hull was intact and undamaged. So why hang around on top of a sandbank waiting for the next high tide to float them off? It was not in Hamilton's nature to sit on his backside and let things happen. He preferred to have the initiative in his own hands, and there seemed to be no good reason why *Rapier* could not be refloated by her own efforts.

"Go over onto the motors, Number One. We should have enough power to pull ourselves off without waiting for the tide." The diesel engines were not geared to give the necessary reverse thrust, so, if he wanted to pull *Rapier* off the shingle, he'd have to use the electric motors.

"Clutches out—switches on." Collis waited for the acknowledgement from the engine compartments in the aft section of the submarine. "Motors grouped down and standing by, sir."

"Full astern both."

Sitting at the control panel in the motor room Chief ERA Jenkins pushed the rheostat control level onto maximum power. The soft hum of the motors rose swiftly to a shrill whine as they strained to the limits of their amperage and the deck plating trembled under the vibration. *Rapier* lurched fitfully as the big bronze propelors bit into the water but she showed no inclination to move. Her bows only dug more firmly into the shingle and she listed slightly to starboard as if too tired to move.

"Stop motors!"

Hamilton could not afford to waste his precious battery reserves for a moment longer than necessary and it did not take him long to realize that *Rapier* was not going to drag herself free under her own power.

"You can open the watertight doors, Number One," he told Collis. "I'm going topsides to see what's happening."

Unfastening the clips of the upper hatch, Hamilton thrust it open and hauled himelf out onto the bridge. He was greeted by the shattering roar of the Blenheim's engines as the bomber swooped across the wavetops at 50 feet toward the stranded submarine. Hamilton took no notice and, with a grin, he grabbed hold of Gilbert's arm and helped him up through the narrow hatchway. He watched the aircraft climbing away into the sun.

"Must be one of the patrol planes I spotted through the periscope after we hit that bloody sandbank," he told the navigator. "Probably checking to make sure we're not in any danger. By the time he gets back to base he'll be boasting that he's rescued a submarine. *And* expect a medal for it."

Ignoring the circling bomber, Hamilton leaned over the side of the bridge to carry out an external inspection of the situation. *Rapier*'s bows were embedded deep in the wet shingle of the sandbank and the dark red paint of her lower hull was exposed with rude clarity. She was lying at an angle and listing slightly to starboard—her weight resting on the curving bulge of the ballast tank. She looked forlorn and helpless but a quick visual inspection confirmed that she was in no danger and Hamilton began estimating the rise of tide necessary to float her off. As she had been running in surface-trim when she hit the sandbank the ballast tanks were already empty so there was nothing he could do to help *Rapier* out of her predicament. Resting his elbows on the armored bridge screen he stared down into the clear green water, watched a crab scuttling sideways across the shingle, and mentally cursed the cruel stroke of fate that had prevented him from catching the fleeing U-boat.

"Jeeesus! What the hell's he trying to do?"

The urgency in Gilbert's voice made Hamilton look up. He was vaguely aware of aircraft engines screaming toward him from the port side and, before he had time to collect his thoughts he heard Ernie Blood's warning shout.

"Hit the deck! The bastard's going to attack!"

As a former petty officer in the Fleet Air Arm the coxswain had seen enough dummy air strikes to recognize the real thing and his warning shout was obeyed by everyone on the bridge—officers and ratings alike diving for the deck without question. The roar of the engines rose to an ear-splitting crescendo as the bomber swept in toward the helpless submarine. Hamilton involuntarily raised his head slightly to peer over the edge of the bridge screen. God Almighty! It was that bloody Blenheim! A mumbling disbelief delayed his reaction for a brief second and then, coming to life, he banged the yeoman on the back.

"On your feet, Groom! Flash our recognition signal! Hurry, man, hurry!"

As Groom's finger tapped a rapid staccato on the trigger of the Aldis lamp Hamilton saw the aircraft alter course.

"Thank God for that," he sighed. "They must have realized who we are. You'd better keep flashing 'em, Groom, just in case."

Blood got up from the deck and joined his skipper at the rails. On the basis of his experience with the swordfish squadrons on *HMS Eagle,* he had read the alteration in the Blenheim's approach run for what it really was.

"Don't be too sure, sir," he yelled in Hamilton's ear. "The pilot's coming in at the wrong angle and he's trying to correct his error. Ten to one he thinks he's attacking a U-boat."

Hamilton saw the bomb doors under the aircraft's belly open and he realized that the coxswain was right. They hadn't been recognized.

"Everyone down!"

The men on the bridge needed no encouragement. And as the Blenheim roared like an express train over the exposed conning tower each man gritted his teeth and waited for the scream of the bombs and the shattering concussion of the explosion that would follow. At that height even the RAF would be unable to miss!

But nothing happened. The noise of the bomber's engine passed directly overhead and began to fade into the sky as the pilot climbed away. No bombs screamed down. The attack was abortive.

Then Hamilton heard the ugly thud of machine-gun bullets striking the thin steel sides of the bridge and the shriek of ricochets whining across the deck. Chief Petty Officer Groom's body jerked, his arms clawed in a rictus of pain, and he rolled over face upwards with his eyes staring blindly at the sky. Blood was coming from three holes in his sweater where the bullets had punched into his chest. Hamilton crawled to the signaller and lifted his head. He saw blood trickling from the man's mouth and he knew there was nothing he could do. Ignoring the danger of another attack he rose to his feet and made for the voicepipe.

"Bridge to control room! Gun crew on deck at the double!" He paused while Collis passed the order back to the waiting men. "And send up two hands to bring Groom down. He bought it when they machine-gunned the bridge."

"Enemy aircraft, sir?" Collis queried. Shut up in the seclusion of the submarine's control room the rest of the Attack Team were ignorant of the events on the surface.

"*Anyone* who attacks my ship is an enemy, Number One."

The gun-layer, followed by Sub-Lieutenant Martindale and the remainder of the gun crew, scrambled up through the conning-tower hatch and hurried down the ladder to the foredeck 3″ high-angle quickfirer. The submarine was canted over at an awkward angle and the base of the gun was awash under several inches of water.

"Open fire as soon as you like," Hamilton shouted to them from the bridge. "Don't wait for any orders. Target circling to port and approaching from stern quarter at 500 feet." He turned away to help the deck party lift Groom's body into the hatch.

Jackson swung open the breech and pushed the first round into place. As he slammed the breech-block shut and pulled down the locking lever he heard Jenkins report that the water-tight plug had been removed from the barrel. Petty Officer Merton quickly sighted the gun toward the stern while Martindale called off the range. Suddenly the bomber tilted onto one wing and the red, white and blue RAF identification roundels painted on the underside gleamed in the fading afternoon sunlight. The sub-lieutenant's face went white as he saw them.

"Hold fire! Check, check, check!" He looked over his shoulder at the bridge. "It's one of ours, sir!" he shouted.

Hamilton's face appeared over the edge of the bridge screen. "I know it is, Mr. Martindale. Unfortunately that fact isn't deterring it from attacking us. Open fire!"

The sub-lieutenant hesitated in an agony of indecision. How *could* they shoot at one of their own aircraft? The Blenheim had had completed its banking turn and, leveling off, it came in on the submarine with flame spurting from the Browning machine-gun in the nose. Realizing that the skipper had no option, and ignoring Martindale's plaintive efforts to stop him, Merton centered his gun-sight and pulled the firing lever.

"Down 100!" he snapped to Jenkins as the shell burst above and behind the approaching aircraft. Jackson thrust another round into the smoking breech and banged down the locking lever.

"Fire!"

Hamilton threw himself flat on the deck as he heard the shrill scream of falling bombs. Pressing his face against the cold steel plating he closed his eyes and prayed.

The thunderclap roar of the exploding bombs deafened the ears and the blast wave sent a wall of black water crashing down over the bridge. Dazed with shock and shivering from the unexpected coldness of the sea water Hamilton shook his head vigorously to clear the ringing noises in his ears. *Rapier* rocked violently under the concussion and her list increased slightly but she seemed otherwise unharmed by her first real taste of war. Hamilton grabbed a stanchion and rose gingerly to his feet to inspect the damage. Even a near miss could prove fatal for a frail vessel like a submarine.

As the Blenheim climbed away the men on the bridge lifted themselves off the deck. Ernie Blood's face was dark with anger and he swore at the departing bomber with a breadth of obscenities that could only be accumulated by twenty years of service on the lower deck. Gilbert, the submarine's navigator, lurched awkwardly as he scrambled to his feet. Blood was seeping from an ugly rip in the left sleeve of his jacket and his arm hung limp and helpless at his side.

"Are you okay, Pilot?" Hamilton asked him.

Gilbert winced but managed to conjure up a weak grin. "Only a scratch, sir. Put me down as 'walking wounded.'"

"Get below and report to Miles," Hamilton told him. "Doc" Miles was *Rapier*'s sick berth attendant. Submarines were not considered important enough to rate a surgeon. He hoped that the doc had enough knowledge to cope. Despite Gilbert's assurance, it looked a nasty wound.

The Blenheim had begun circling for another attack and as Hamilton helped the navigator into the upper hatch he realized that *Rapier*'s deck gun was silent. Cursing the over-cautious Martindale he hurried to the front of the bridge to find out what was going on. He'd have to deal with that young man when they got out of this mess. Reaching the forward edge of the conning-tower upperworks he peered over the screen. The gun crew had vanished. *And so had the gun!*

All that remained was a gaping hole in the deck plating. The blast of the bombs had wrenched the one-ton weapon from its mounting as cleanly as a dentist removing a decayed tooth from a patient's jaw. Merton, the gun-layer, lay sprawled on the upper curve of the starboard ballast tank like a limp rag doll, and, floating twenty feet from the side of the submarine, and drifting astern in the current, Jackson's body bobbed face down in the red water. There was no sign of Jenkins or the sub-lieutenant. They had either been blown to pieces by the exploding bomb or swept over the side and drowned.

There was no trace of sentiment in Hamilton's reaction to the tragedy. The four men could be replaced. But, deprived of her single anti-aircraft gun, *Rapier* was now defenseless against the renewed onslaught of the bomber. He bent over the voicepipe.

"Bring our two Vickers to the bridge, Number One. The deck gun's been knocked out. We'll have to fight it out with machine-guns!"

"Captain, sir! Look at *this!*"

Hamilton spun around in response to the coxswain's incredulous shout. Good God! As if they hadn't enough to cope with already. What bloody chance did they stand now?

The U-boat had surfaced. *And it was steaming straight toward them with its deck guns manned and ready to open fire.*

"If you know any prayers, Chief, you'd better start saying 'em," he told the coxswain.

Leading Seaman Woodward appeared through the hatch, pushed the Vicker's machine-gun onto the deck plating, and heaved himself out onto the bridge. Ambridge followed close behind with the second gun clasped to his chest. Hamilton ordered them to the port and starboard bridge wings. There was no time to clamp the guns into their traversing rings and he made no attempt to hurry the two men. They'd jump quick enough once they realized what was at stake. The Blenheim completed its turn and leveled off for its next bombing run.

The sharp crack of gunfire ripped the air like torn calico snapping in a gale and Hamilton ducked instinctively in anticipation of the U-boat's first salvo. But the sound of the bursting shells seemed curiously far away and something prompted him to look skywards. Two black puffs of cordite smoke spread lazily in the breeze just astern of the Blenheim and the aircraft jinked wildly to avoid the shell splinters. The U-boat's guns fired again and this time the shell bursts bracketed the weaving bomber with ominous accuracy. Two more salvoes followed in quick succession and he saw a wisp of petrol vapor and glycol stream from the Blenheim's starboard engine.

Hamilton could only conclude that the whole world had gone crazy. First *Rapier* had come under attack from a friendly aircraft. And now, as a crowning madness, a German submarine was coming to its rescue. If he hadn't seen it with his own eyes he would never have believed it. And, having seen it, he could certainly never explain it.

The Blenheim was fast losing height as, trailing black smoke from the starboard wing, it disappeared from sight behind the mudbanks. Hamilton watched the German guns being lowered from their high-angle elevation as the U-boat turned away and he assumed, with objective calmness, that they were preparing for surface action. Leading Seaman Woodward obviously thought the same and, slotting the Vickers into its mounting, he pulled back the bolt. Hamilton turned sharply.

"Hold your fire, Woodward," he ordered. And, even as he gave the unexpected order, he wondered what was possessing him to yield up his only opportunity of snatching the initiative at the beginning of the battle. Picking up his binoculars he examined the submarine as it passed along *Rapier*'s beam at less than a mile distance. What the devil were they up to? The guns had been secured in the fore-and-aft position and the crews were climbing back up the ladder into the conning-tower. As he stared through his glasses he saw an officer wearing a white-topped cap, presumably the U-boat's commander, raise his hand in a valedictory wave. Then fountains of frothing water erupted along the length of the submarine, her bows angled down sharply, and she slid quietly beneath the surface.

"Well I'll be damned," Ernie Blood said in disbelief. "And to think I never believed in fairy godmothers!"

Hamilton grinned. He could have found a far more expressive way of putting it.

"Have you taken leave of your senses, Lieutenant?" Grenson demanded as he threw Hamilton's Report of Proceedings down on the desk with an angry gesture. "I've never heard such preposterous rubbish in my life."

"I can assure you every single word is true, sir," Hamilton protested.

"Are you seriously trying to tell me that an enemy U-boat came to the surface in order to save you from a further bombing attack?"

"That's how it happened, sir. And I can produce several witnesses to confirm what I saw."

Grenson glowered down at the report. He considered Hamilton to blame for the escape of the U-boat and for the abysmal failure of his elaborate scheme to ambush the enemy submarine. If the damned young fool hadn't run himself aground Hitler would now have one less U-boat. The plan had been foolproof but, thanks to an inexperienced half-blind RAF pilot and an inept submarine commander, he now found himself at the center of an inter-service row that threatened to reach the ears of the War Cabinet itself.

"Very well, Lieutenant," he said slowly. "Let's take your fanciful story step by step. You ran your submarine onto a sandbank. Was that just bad luck or merely bad seamanship?"

"Neither, sir. The charts showed a channel through the sandbank with adequate depth of water for *Rapier* to pass over in surface trim."

"But the U-boat not only crossed the same sandbank safely—it crossed it in a submerged position."

"Yes, sir. I've known similar things happen when I've been yacht racing along that particular stretch of coast. The channels can change position and depth with every tide. It just happened that the enemy skipper guessed right."

141

Grenson dropped his pencil on the desk. His initial annoyance was fading. He knew that Hamilton was not the sort of person to invent such a story to cover up for his own mistakes. And, as he had pointed out, he could produce witnesses.

"Very well," he continued. "The charts were misleading. We'll pass that point for the moment. When did the U-boat come to the surface?"

"Soon after the second air attack, sir. I would say almost immediately after we lost the deck gun. The enemy commander must have realized we had no means of defense."

"Or," Grenson pointed out logically, "it might have been sheer coincidence. And why shouldn't he open fire on the Blenheim? After all, so far as *he* was concerned, it *was* an enemy aircraft."

"I quite agree, sir. But you're overlooking one fact. He didn't *have* to surface. And why, having chased off the Blenheim, did he submerge again without attacking *Rapier*. We were a sitting target."

Grenson remained silent. He still found it impossible to accept Hamilton's story; there seemed no plausible explanation for the action of the U-boat. He could only conclude that it must have been a matter of mistaken identities all around—a not unusual situation for men facing combat for the first time. He slipped the offending report into a blue file.

"I suggest we let the matter go no further, Hamilton. I do not accept your account and I am sure there is some logical explanation of what happened. Will you kindly draft another report. And this time I want facts and not fancies. Just say precisely what happened and don't elaborate into theory. Is that clear?"

"Yes, sir."

Grenson walked to the window and stared out in silence for a few moments.

"I will see that Lieutenant Gilbert's notes on the chart errors are passed onto the Hydrographer's Department." He turned away from the window and sat down behind his desk again. "Meanwhile we've got to get *Rapier* seaworthy. What's the score?"

"It's mostly superficial damage to the outer casing, sir. The pressure hull is okay. Jacobs says he can patch up the bullet holes inside twelve hours. It's the gun that'll take the time. Apparently they've got to bring one by road from Chatham. And even then Jacobs is doubtful whether he has the facilities for mounting it."

Grenson's worried expression deepened. He tapped his pencil absently on the desk as he digested the news. "There's only one thing for it, Hamilton," he said finally. "We'll have to get the dockyard to weld a plate over the mounting and you must go to sea without a gun. I can't spare *Rapier* for more than 24 hours while this new panic's on."

Hamilton shrugged. "That's okay by me, sir. I often wonder why they bother to waste money fitting deck guns on submarines; we never get the chance to use them. It might have been a good idea in the last war. But these days, with the danger of air attack, no one in his right mind comes to the surface. It wouldn't bother me if they never put the gun back."

Grenson glanced up at him. *Rapier*'s skipper obviously had no idea what *Operation Manhunt* involved.

"You know that *Koenig* has scuttled herself?" he asked suddenly.

Hamilton nodded. He'd heard the news over the radio a few days earlier. It hadn't really concerned him at the time although, naturally, he was glad to learn that both *Graf Spee* and *Koenig* had now been accounted for. A pity they'd scuttled themselves and denied the Royal Navy the chance of finishing them off in battle. But *Graf Spee*, at least, had been given a good hammering by Commodore Harwood's cruisers before her final humiliation. He wondered what the hell the two pocket-battleships had to do with the next operation.

"Scuttling is not the end of the story so far as the navy is concerned," Grenson elaborated. "Both raiders had a tanker in company which was used as a prison ship for the crews of the ships they destroyed. *Graf Spee*'s back-up ship was *Altmark*. *Koenig* had *Nordsee* in support. Both ships went into hiding after the battleships were sunk but we've now received reliable intelligence reports that they intend to make a dash for home. We know *Altmark* is somewhere inside the Arctic Circle to the north of Iceland and the C-in-C Home

Fleet has allocated a destroyer flotilla to pick her up as soon as she's spotted."*

Grenson paused and lit his pipe. He glanced at Hamilton to see his reaction.

"With nearly 300 men to be rescued *Altmark* will have to be a destroyer job. But *Nordsee* has, to the best of our knowledge, only a dozen prisoners on board and the first lord has given the Harwich Flotilla the task of rescuing them. It's a bit of a cloak-and-dagger operation because we'll be working inside Norwegian territorial waters—that's why it's been given to the submarines. I gather the Foreign Office are totally opposed to the use of surface forces but, in view of the number of men involved, they've had to give way over the *Altmark* end of the operation. Obviously the last thing we want to do is to violate Norwegian neutrality in case Hitler uses it as an excuse to invade Norway. So, as you can see, it's a delicate little scheme. And there'll be no question of using torpedoes—not unless you want to kill a dozen of our own people."

"You mean we've got to lie submerged inside Norwegian territorial waters and try to ambush the prison ship?" Grenson nodded and Hamilton continued, "But if we're not to torpedo it what *are* we intended to do?"

"Board it."

Hamilton raised his eyebrows. "With a submarine?"

"Yes, Lieutenant."

"But don't forget, sir, *Rapier* won't have a gun."

Grenson shrugged. "I appreciate the difficulties, Lieutenant, but there is no alternative. We expect *Nordsee* to make its move in the next seven days and that doesn't leave time for *Rapier* to go down to Chatham for another weapon. You'll have to manage. Remember the motto over the door at Dartmouth— *There is nothing the navy cannot do.*"

Hamilton was about to remind his flotilla commander that he had been promoted from the lower deck. In fact he'd never been inside Dartmouth Naval College in his entire career. But he decided it might not

* *Altmark* was ultimately boarded by Captain Phillip Vian's *Cossack* in Josing Fjord on February 16, 1940. 299 British prisoners were rescued.

be diplomatic. And, unaware of Hamilton's thoughts, Grenson changed the subject.

"You'll need some crew replacements," he said.

Hamilton nodded. "You'll find a copy of the *S.1121* attached to my report, sir. And I've sent off the admiralty telegram. We lost the fourth hand, the gunner's mate and two seamen gunners, plus a yeoman of signals. And, of course, Gilbert was wounded although, fortunately, he's been passed fit for duty."

"The replacements are in hand. Sub-Lieutenant Evans is being drafted straight from Greenwich. The admiralty is cutting the current course short to make up for losses. He'll have to qualify while he's on active service. Once we get the RNVR boys trained we'll be able to send the regulars back to school to finish off. But until then they'll have to shift for themselves."

Hamilton didn't envy the young sub-lieutenant his task. He could recall sweating blood over the Greenwich course himself some few year's back. He listened attentively as Grenson continued.

"I've managed to grab an old yeoman of signals who was pensioned off last year and the rear admiral has agreed to replace the other three. You won't get qualified gunners, of course, but as you won't have a gun I don't suppose it will matter very much."

Hamilton made no comment. Manning the submarine was not his problem. He simply had to take what he was given and be thankful.

"When do you want me to leave, sir?" he asked.

Grenson glanced at his desk calendar. "Wednesday at the latest. On the morning tide. That will give the dockyard time to weld a plate over the foredeck gun mounting and patch up the other holes."

Two whole days! Hamilton knew he had plenty to do but, even so, it was an unexpected bonus. He wondered whether he dared ask.

"Do you think I could have a 12 hour pass, sir? Collis can get *Rapier* into dock for the repairs and I'd be back in good time to put the new men through their paces."

Grenson smiled understandingly and nodded. "I think it could be arranged, Lieutenant. Going to see Keble-Hampshire's girl, I suppose?"

145

Hamilton looked puzzled. With a seat on the board, Admiral Keble-Hampshire was one of the most powerful men in the navy. How the devil was an impecunious junior officer with no social connections ever likely to meet the sixth sea lord's daughter? Grenson misread the expression on his face.

"No need to be embarrassed, Lieutenant," he grinned. "Young Caroline would be a tremendous catch for any ambitious officer."

Hamilton felt his blood freeze. God Almighty! He'd had Caroline in bed twice without knowing who she was. That bloody fool Cavendish should have warned him. But surely old Grenson was getting things mixed up.

"No, sir. It's not Admiral Keble-Hampshire's daughter. Her name's Faversham——Caroline Faversham." In fact Hamilton had no intentions of wasting his precious 12 hours pass on Second-bloody-Officer Faversham now that he had met Rita. But he thought he ought to clear up the misunderstanding before it caused any embarrassment.

"That's the one," Grenson beamed. "She's really the admiral's stepdaughter and she stuck to her father's surname when her mother remarried."

Hamilton shared the joke with a shamefaced smile. But, underneath, he wasn't laughing. What the hell was he going to do? It was bad enough finding out that he'd been knocking off an admiral's daughter. But dropping her in favor of a barmaid was not exactly the best way of furthering his career. Not that he was going to let *that* stop him from seeing Rita.

Who the hell cared about a career anyway when there was a war on? He'd probably be dead by this time next year—perhaps even sooner. And so far as Hamilton was concerned Admiral Keble-Hampshire could do to himself precisely what *he'd* been doing to his step-daughter!

# CHAPTER NINE

"Acting Sub-Lieutenant Evans, sir. Reporting for duty as fourth hand."

Hamilton passed a hand across his eyes and wished that people would learn not to shout. The clanging noise of the dockyard engineers working on the outer hull reverberated inside the boat and every bang of their hammers sent a red hot knife lancing through his aching head. Three cups of scalding black coffee had failed to neutralize the foul taste in his mouth and he was feeling decidedly delicate. Drinking, he concluded, didn't get rid of problems. It only brought fresh ones.

Putting his pen down on the desk he looked up at the sub-lieutenant. Well, he was young—probably too young—but he looked keen enough. Hamilton paused. There was something very familiar about the new officer's face but he couldn't place it. The mental effort of remembering only made his headache worse and he scowled blackly.

"Welcome aboard, Mr. Evans." The greeting sounded coldly routine and insincere. Hamilton hated the mandatory chat with which a commanding officer was expected to welcome a new officer. With less than 24 hours left to sailing he had a hundred and one things to attend to. "What experience do you have?"

"Virtually none, sir," Evans said with cheerful truthfulness. "I did a seven day crash course at Blockhouse on technical theory and another couple of weeks on a training boat learning the practical side. In fact I only shipped my stripe two months ago."

"You've been pulled off the Greenwich course I understand," Hamilton observed. The aspirin and black coffee were holding his headache at bay and he was beginning to feel a little more human. He started to fill his pipe as he searched his memory to remember where he had seen Evans before. "You'll find it tough going trying to study while you're a watch-keeping officer. The juniors have to carry out full duties—no room for passengers in a submarine, you know."

147

"I'll cope, sir," Evans told him with the easy optimism of youth. "Fortunately I got a second in seamanship before I left Greenwich. So I should be able to pull my weight."

Hamilton nodded. The new fourth hand might be only partially trained but he looked promising material. Humility was never a common attribute amongst sublieutenants. "What have you served in?" he asked more to make conversation than because he wanted to know. The details of Evans' career would be in the Establishment File when it arrived from the flotilla paymaster's office later in the day.

"Well, sir, I started in *Calypso* when I left Dartmouth. Then I did a spell in the West Indies with *Diomede*. After that I was in *Leviathan* with the Home Fleet."

Hamilton sat up suddenly. *Leviathan*. Of *course*! Evans was the midshipman who'd escorted him to Admiral Robertson's quarters when he'd been summoned on board the flagship with *Surge*'s logbook. It was only eighteen months since Cavendish had launched his madcap attack on the German Fleet and yet it seemed like an age.

"Good God! Bonzo!"

Evans grinned ruefully. "I was hoping I'd heard the last of that particular nickname, sir." He stared hard at Hamilton's face and recognition dawned with equal suddenness. "Well I'm damned. Weren't you first officer of Gerry Cavendish's boat when we had that bust-up at Kiel?"

"I certainly was. And I won't forget you in a hurry either, Sub. I think you were the only friendly face I met that day. Take a seat and I'll give you a quick run down on your duties. I shall be tied up with paperwork for the next few hours but Collis, my number one, will take you around the boat and introduce you to everyone." Hamilton rummaged amongst the papers piled on top of his miniscule desk and emerged with a dogeared duty roster. "As fourth hand you'll be generally assisting with watch-keeping although, so far as possible, you'll only be officer of the watch in an emergency. During diving stations your normal position will be in the fore-ends with the torpedoes and, in the event of a surface action, you're responsible for the deck gun. Only you won't be on this trip because we don't happen to have one at the moment."

"So I noticed, sir. But I'm not bad with a pea-shooter."

"Don't laugh too soon," Hamilton warned him grimly. "We're in for a rough trip. If I were you," he added with an impish grin, "I'd get in some practice with my catapult as well."

He glanced at his wristwatch and decided regretfully that he'd have to bring the interview to a close. He stood up and held out his hand. The sub-lieutenant grasped it firmly.

"Good to have you with us, Mr. Evans."

And this time he meant it.


Hamilton felt no undue surprise at finding Commander Mason sitting in Grenson's office when he arrived for the final briefing. The DNI's assistant had an odd habit of popping up in unexpected places and he would certainly have an interest in Operation Manhunt. In many ways he was more surprised at not finding a representative of the Foreign Office present. But presumably the DNI's department had been delegated the task of keeping an eye on the diplomatic implications. Closing the door behind him he turned to Captain Grenson and saluted.

"Sit down, Hamilton. You already know Commander Mason, I believe?"

Hamilton nodded curtly to the other officer. "Good morning, sir. We met at Rear Admiral Mabberly's conference in December if I remember correctly."

"I certainly remember you, Lieutenant," Mason acknowledged coldly and Hamilton sensed that, for some reason, he had still not been fully cleared by the DNI. He wanted to ask Mason if there was any further news about Cavendish's death but decided it would not be politic to revive old wounds. Pulling a chair forward he sat down.

"I've already given you a brief outline of *Manhunt*," Grenson began. "The Harwich submarines are forming a patrol line *inside* Norwegian territorial waters with a view to intercepting the prison ship *Nordsee*. Your boat will be the last to leave so you'll have to take the southernmost station." Turning to the wallchart he pointed to the line of longitude 61° N in the vicinity of Sogne Soen. "This will be your area of operation. *Starfish* will be to the north of the Romsdall Islands and the others are strung along the coast as far as the Lofotens."

"I see, sir. I'll be a sort of long stop."

"That's about it," Grenson nodded. "We don't really expect *Nordsee* to get as far south as your billet but you'll be England's last hope if she does." He sat down again. "You will, of course, be given written orders but I want to stress the importance of not showing yourself in Norwegian waters unless you are forced to. You will remain submerged throughout the day and will proceed outside the three-mile limit each night to surface and recharge batteries. *H-86* from the Scapa Flotilla will take over your patrol area while you're away." He took a heavily sealed envelope from the drawer of his desk and handed it to Hamilton. "You'll find all the routine instructions, signal times, and codes in that. Now I'll pass you over to Commander Mason."

Mason subjected Hamilton to a cold, searching stare before he spoke. Then, shifting slightly in his chair, he took over from Grenson.

"This is a highly important operation from both a military and a diplomatic viewpoint, Lieutenant. One of the prisoners on *Nordsee* is an Austrian-born physicist with, I am given to understand, an international reputation in his own special field of work. It is the unanimous opinion of the War Cabinet that he must be taken off the ship before it reaches Germany. So far as international security is concerned *Nordsee* is a far more important target than *Altmark*. And this is why we are using submarines for the job. Churchill* is prepared to send destroyers to rescue the *Altmark* prisoners and, in the view of the Foreign Office, such action could easily lead to a shooting match with Norwegian gunboats. In the case of the *Nordsee* we cannot

* At this period of the war Winston Churchill was First Lord of the Admiralty.

afford to take such a risk. And, for the same reason, there must be no slip-ups."

"I understand, sir."

"You will only board the tanker if she is inside the 3-mile limit. If she is sailing outside you are to advise the SNO 18th Flotilla by radio. The destroyers will be patroling along the line, latitude 4°E and they will have no difficulty in picking her up."

"What happens if the Norwegian Navy intervenes, sir?" Hamilton asked.

"If there is no other way—sink them!"

"But won't that trigger off an international incident? I thought that was precisely what we were trying to avoid."

Mason's face was completely devoid of expression. "It probably will, Lieutenant," he agreed. "But that is the War Cabinet's worry—not yours. You have full authority to take whatsoever action is necessary to ensure the rescue of the prisoners." He paused for further questions but Hamilton shook his head. "There is just one more thing. You are on no account to attack any other ships while engaged on this mission. There is a total embargo on all offensive action until such time as the codeword *Bloodhound* is transmitted." Mason leaned forward to emphasize the point. "And that means *every* enemy ship, Lieutenant, including U-boats."

"I appreciate the need for secrecy, sir. Obviously it would be unwise to reveal our presence by attacking enemy ships before the rescue is completed. But once it's over surely there will be no objection if we attack any likely targets we see?"

"You will attack *nothing*, Lieutenant. This is a specific directive from Section VI. Even the DNI has been given no reason. But in the navy we do as we are told. No enemy ship or U-boat is to be attacked during this operation unless you receive the clearance codeword *Bloodhound*." Hamilton could feel the commander's hooded eyes staring at him. "After the way that U-boat came to your rescue last week I would have expected you to welcome such an instruction." There was no mistaking the sarcasm in his voice and Hamilton flushed. So, despite Grenson's assurances, his Report of Proceedings had been passed on to Intelligence. They must think him a fine fool.

Having had time to consider the strange incident of the U-boat at Sunk Sand, Hamilton now realized that Grenson had been right. It had been his first experience of full-scale combat and, in the heat of the moment, it was easy to imagine things happening when, in fact, they didn't. Not that there was any doubt about the U-boat surfacing. Nor opening fire and driving off the Blenheim. But in the confused stress of battle it was not difficult to misinterpret motives.

In the quiet calm of the depot-ship's wardroom he had seen things in perspective. There had been nothing altruistic in the enemy captain's actions. He had shot up the Blenheim for the sole reason that it was an enemy aircraft. And, with time against him, he had passed over the chance of attacking *Rapier* so that he could make good his escape before the escort forces arrived on the scene. And, having realized he'd made a fool of himself, Hamilton now bitterly regretted his over-hasty report. The Germans called it *blechkoller*—tin disease—the hysteria brought about by the strain of fighting a war in the claustrophobic confines of a tin-can coffin.

"You read my report, sir?" he asked Mason.

The commander nodded. He made no comment.

"Was it passed on to Section VI?"

Mason nodded again. "Any unusual behavior by enemy submarines is automatically passed on as a matter of routine." He paused, as if uncertain whether to commit himself further. "For some reason or another Section VI didn't seem very surprised. God knows why. It was the most ludicrous story I've ever heard in my life."

Hamilton nodded his agreement. "I'm afraid I made a fool of myself, sir. But after a combat action the imagination tends to work overtime and I was still under stress when I made my report to Captain Grenson. It was the first time I've ever lost any of my men."

Mason's expression softened fractionally. "I understand how you felt, Lieutenant. I haven't forgotten my own reaction after my first taste of enemy gunfire. I think that, so far as flotilla is concerned, and the DNI as well for that matter, we can regard the incident as closed." He shrugged. "But I'm damned if I can understand Section VI's attitude."

"They're always the same," Grenson observed sourly. "They just happen to know more about certain things than we do. The galling part is that *we* have to do what *they* tell us."

"Ours not to reason why, old boy," Mason murmured.

Grenson nodded. "Ours but to do . . ."

". . . or die."

Hamilton picked up his sealed orders, replaced his cap, and saluted. Somehow he didn't like the pointed way the two senior officers were looking at him as he left the room.

Collis was waiting at the head of the gangway as Hamilton returned to the quayside and boarded *Rapier*. Having saluted the quarterdeck he glanced down at the newly repaired hull plating. The submarine looked naked without her quick-firer but, from a practical point of view, the absence of the encumbering lump of metal should add a good two knots to her underwater speed. And Hamilton had a strange feeling that, once committed to *Operation Manhunt*, he'd be glad to have it.

"We'll be leaving on the afternoon tide, Number One. Are all stores aboard and secured?"

"Yes, sir." Collis paused. "There's just one thing, sir. The RNAD superintendent has delivered another two machine-guns and a crate of rifles. And they've given us a rubber dinghy." He pointed aft and Hamilton could see the bulbous black raft lashed to the deck plating behind the conning-tower. "What the devil do we want all this extra gear for, sir?"

Hamilton smiled enigmatically. "Haven't you heard, Number One? They want us to go whale hunting to help out with the meat ration. Next time out we're getting a harpoon gun. And a diver to go down for oysters!"

"Captain to the control room!"

Hamilton groaned wearily, swung his legs out of the bunk, grabbed his cap, and hurried to the control room in his stockinged feet. False alarms occurred with monotonous regularity but every sighting had to be thoroughly checked out. And the importance of the operation meant that responsibility could be delegated to no one but himself.

It was the beginning of the third day's patrol. They had changed places with *H-86* thirty minutes earlier as the pink fingers of dawn reached over the rim of the snow-capped mountains edging the fjords that bit deep into the Norwegian coastline. And everything seemed set for another twelve hours of deadening boredom as *Rapier* ceaselessly quartered her patrol area inside the 3-mile limit. Apart from the duty watch the men spent their time reading and sleeping but, for the submarine's handful of officers, there was little time for relaxation. Each man took a one-hour stint at the periscope while the back-up team stood by for instant action if the quarry was sighted.

At precisely fifteen minutes past each hour Hamilton brought *Rapier* to a position just below the surface so that the radio aerials could reach up clear of the sea to receive any urgent signals. Then, having maintained a listening watch for exactly two minutes, the submarine slid back to periscope depth and the monotonous patrol routine was continued.

"One minute to radio time, sir," Collis told Hamilton as he entered the control room. Hamilton nodded and leaned against the bulkhead. He watched the sweep second hand of the chronometer jerk rhythmically toward the apex of the dial.

"Level at 10 feet, Number One. Stand by for signals. Take her up."

"Up 'planes. Steady at 10 feet, Cox'n."

*Rapier* glided silently upwards and as she reached the required depth Tropp neutralized the big diving wheel while Ernie Blood carefully leveled the submarine off with the stern hydroplanes.

"Ten feet, sir. Trimmed level. Nothing in sight."

"Stand by."

The control room went quiet as they waited. They had carried out the same routine twenty-four times in

154

the process of the patrol. And on each occasion their anxious wait had gone unrewarded. No one expected it to be any different this time but, inevitably, tension grew as Murray tuned his apparatus into the special traffic-free waveband allocated for *Operation Manhunt*. They saw the radio operator lean forward as he picked something up in his headset. His left hand moved the tuning knob a fraction and he reached for the signal pad.

Hamilton pushed himself away from the bulkhead and waited expectantly beside the receiver as the message emerged letter by letter. Despite the code, he recognized the prefix immediately and snapped his fingers at Evans to bring him the cypher book. Peering over Murray's shoulder he began decoding the signal while the operator continued writing down the morse groups.

*Immediate. Manhunt. To Mayflower. (Mayflower was Rapier's codename while the operation was in progress.) Nordsee passed Namos Point at 09-52 GMT. Course SSE inside 3-mile limit. Speed 12 knots. Funnel repainted in Greek Line colors. Now sailing as Olympus of Athens.*

"Where the hell do they get their information from?" Hamilton asked no one in particular as he read out the decoded signal.

Collis shrugged. He wasn't very interested. All that mattered to him was whether the information was accurate. It was Murray, the radio operator, who seemed the most puzzled. He swung his seat away from the receiver.

"Sir?"

"Yes, Murray?"

The radio operator hesitated as if afraid of sounding silly. But he knew it was his duty to put the skipper in the picture. He took the plunge.

"I'd swear that signal only came from a transmitter about twelve miles away. You get to estimating distances on the basis of signal strength in this job," he added by way of explanation.

Hamilton was suddenly alert. Perhaps the message had come from a shore station, a coast-watcher in-

155

stalled by Intelligence to check German shipping moving inside Norwegian territorial waters.

"It was probably repeated onto us by one of the destroyers," he told Murray. "They're patroling approximately twelve miles to seaward."

Murray shook his head. "No, sir. It wasn't a repeated signal. There would have been the usual indication if it was." He hesitated again and then dropped his bombshell. "I'd say it was sent on a *Telefunken* transmitter."

"A German Navy transmitter?"

"Yes, sir. I can recognize the characteristics. I used to monitor enemy wireless traffic when I was at Rosyth."

Hamilton paused. Perhaps the Germans had discovered the secret of *Operation Manhunt* and were using a false message to take the submarine on a wild goose chase in pursuit of an innocently neutral vessel while *Nordsee* ran clear of the ambush. The total lack of news over the previous 48 hours suggested she had already evaded the other submarines and, in that case, *Rapier* would be her last hurdle. Yet how *could* the enemy have discovered not only the secret wavelength but also the pre-arranged signal time? Despite the imposition of wireless silence, Hamilton *had* to know the answer.

"Call up command," he told Murray. "Ask them if Signal 10-16 of today re *Olympus* is confirmed. I'll stay at this depth until you receive a reply."

As Murray began tapping our *Rapier*'s call-sign Hamilton sat down in his canvas stool to consider this latest turn of events. Until he received a reply from Harwich he had to proceed on the basis that the message, however suspicious, was authentic. There was no time to do anything else. If the tanker had passed Namos Point at 09.52 and was running at 12 knots she would be in visual contact within the next ten minutes.

Now that he had finally come face to face with the reality of the situation for the first time Hamilton suddenly realized the near impossibility of his task. Without a gun he had no weapon with which to stop the prison ship. And even if he succeeded in stopping her, *Rapier*'s low freeboard made it impossible to board the

156

high-sided hull of a tanker in ballast. Why the hell did Churchill have to meddle and insist on using submarines, he thought angrily. It was a job for the destroyers. If they were prepared to authorize Vian's flotilla to violate Norwegian neutrality in order to board *Altmark* what the hell did another violation matter?

"Reply from Harwich, sir."

Hamilton nodded, took the signal slip, and hurriedly decoded the brief message.

*Immediate. Manhunt. Warder to Mayflower. Signal 10-16 of today confirmed. Source reliable. Warder. 10-27.*

So Murray had been right. The information about *Nordsee*'s change of identity had not originated from Harwich. But if it hadn't derived from admiralty sources where the hell *had* it come from?

"Take her down to periscope depth, Number One."

Hamilton had no firm plan of action in mind but he was not prepared to admit it to anyone, not even Collis. The men trusted him. And it was a trust he dared not betray. He swung the lens of the periscope toward the craggy coastline and searched along the rocks.

"Boarding party prepare to embark. Deck watch to stand by." The men crowded into the control room with their boots and weapons clattering noisily on the bare deck plating. They looked slightly incongruous with their steel helmets and canvas gaiters and Hamilton felt a little like an infantry commander about to send his men "over the top" at zero hour. He turned to Gilbert.

"You're in charge of the dinghy, Pilot. As soon as the boat is launched make for the rocks and keep out of sight. When I fire a green flare I want you to come alongside the disengaged side of the tanker and board her."

"Is that what the grappling hooks are for, sir?"

"Yes. It's primitive but it's all we have. You will lead the boarding party itself. Evans and Woodward are to remain in the dinghy."

"But how the hell are you going to stop her in the first place?" Collis asked. "She'll blow us out of the water as soon as we surface."

Hamilton shook his head. "No she won't, Number

157

One. Assuming our intelligence is reliable German auxiliary tankers are not armed. That's why they can sail inside neutral waters without breaking international law. In all probability they've go no more weapons on board than we have—a few machine-guns and a couple of dozen rifles. So if it comes to a fight the odds will be even. And I'd put my money on the navy in a fair scrap any day."

The men grinned. Hamilton knew how to build up their confidence and he saw some of the pre-combat tension clear from their faces.

"As to your first question, Number One," he continued. "I think a little *ruse de guerre* is permissible in the circumstances." He turned to Watson. "Do you have a swastika ensign in your locker, Yeoman?"

"I think so, sir."

"Good man. Bring it to the control room." As yeoman of signals ducked through the circular opening in the forward bulkhead Hamilton grinned at the circle of expectant faces gathered around him. "Just over a week ago we were mistaken for a U-boat by the RAF. If it can happen once there is no reason why we cannot make it happen again. When we come to the surface I intend to run up the Nazi flag and, with luck, *Nordsee* will fall for it." He paused for a moment. "If we're going to pull this stunt off successfully it will mean taking chances. There must be nothing visible that might identify us as a British submarine. So although we may be under fire I cannot permit anyone on deck to wear a steel helmet. Are the duty watch willing to go up on the bridge without any form of head protection?"

There was a general murmur of agreement and Hamilton knew he need have no fears about the spirit of his men.

"Excuse me, sir. I've got a *Kriegsmarine* hat I picked up at Kiel last year," Lloyd piped up hesitantly. "Would it be of any use?"

"You bet it will, lad." Hamilton looked around the circle of men. "Now does anyone here speak fluent German?"

"I do, sir."

Jimmy Harper, the ex-chorus boy, raised his arm diffidently.

"Good for you, Harper. I'll explain what I want you to do later. Now—are there any questions?"

Collis cleared his throat. "Just one thing, sir. According to International Law we are supposed to run up our true colors before we actually open fire. But you only told the Yeoman to bring a swastika' ensign. Shouldn't we have the White Ensign as well?"

Hamilton shook his head. "We're already contravening International Law by attacking an enemy ship in neutral waters, Number One. And we're doing that on direct orders from the War Cabinet. I'm not prepared to do anything which is likely to place either my boat or my men at risk. And if I have to break the law on my own account I'm quite happy to do so. I shall be in good company. The Nazi flag will therefore remain flying until the operation is completed. There's no knowing who or what might turn up once we've started and a bit of confusion won't do anyone any harm!"

Collis grinned his approval. He wasn't questioning the skipper's orders. Like any other conscientious executive officer he was only trying to ensure nothing had been overlooked.

"I understand, sir. You can count on us to back you up—even if we have to stand to attention on deck and sing the bloody German National Anthem!"

*Kapitan* Dührer was already thinking about the welcome he would receive when he docked at Kiel. After a journey of over 10,000 miles *Nordsee* was a mere 48 hours away from the Fatherland. What could possibly go wrong now? With her false name, her newly painted funnel bands, and the Greek mercantile ensign streaming from the jackstaff on her poop, she looked the epitome of an innocent neutral as she made her way cautiously down the Norwegian coast safely inside the 3-mile limit.

Dührer had good reason to feel confident in the ultimate success of his mission. A Norwegian gunboat which had stopped and searched the ship off Stavanger had found nothing. And the noisy rattle of a steam winch on the forecastle had effectively deadened the shouts of the prisoners locked inside the empty No. 3 storage tank. *Nordsee* was flying her correct national

159

colors and there had been no necessity for lies or evasions. As an unarmed merchant ship she had every right to proceed inside neutral waters and the Norwegian boarding officer had stamped their papers with a cheery smile.

There had been a submarine alarm the same day but *Nordsee*'s superior speed enabled her to get away with ease although Dührer experienced a momentary feeling of surprise that a British submarine would dare to attack shipping inside the territorial waters of a so-called friendly neutral. So that evening, as an added precaution, *Nordsee* was taken into a lonely fjord. And when she emerged from her temporary lair the following morning a few pots of paint had transformed her into an innocent Greek tanker.

Her newly acquired identity had been subjected to its first test less than eight hours later when a British submarine surfaced and fired a warning shot across her bows. Dührer's impersonation of an enraged Greek skipper had been a masterpiece of the thespian arts. He swore. He gesticulated. And he danced up and down on the bridge in feigned anger while the submarine drifted closer and its commander demanded details of the ship's identity over his loud-hailer. But the bluff had worked and, after fifteen tense minutes of argument, the submarine turned away and submerged. Dührer was delighted with his success. And he was even more delighted with the free bottle of Scotch whisky which the Englishman had sent across to placate the enraged "neutral" skipper.

"Submarine surfacing one mile off starbord bow, *Herr Kapitan*."

Dührer raised his powerful Zeiss binoculars and swore softly. Although success had bolstered his confidence he did not relish a repetition of the previous day's charade.

"I think it's one of our U-boats, *Herr Kapitan*," First Officer Eckhardt reported. He turned to *Nordsee*'s quartermaster. "Slow ahead both."

Dührer was not so certain. And he hadn't brought *Nordsee* half across the world by wild guesswork. "Negative, Quartermaster. Maintain course and speed. Remember we're a Greek ship. There could be hidden eyes up on those cliffs watching every movement we make."

The submarine was now fully surfaced and a stiff breeze crackled the blood-red Nazi ensign flying boldly from her conning-tower jackstaff. Dührer watched with narrowed eyes as the vessel altered course toward the tanker. He knew of only one U-boat designated to operate in this particular area and this submarine was a stranger.

"Ahoy *Nordsee*!" *Rapier*'s powerful loud-hailer carried Able Seaman Harper's voice across the rolling gray sea and the shout was clearly audible to the men on the tanker's bridge. "*U-35* to *Nordsee*. Ahoy there!"

Dührer made no use of the tanker's own loud-hailer. He played the part of the Greek down to the smallest detail. Picking up a megaphone he stood in the corner of the bridge wing and replied in English.

"Not *Nordsee*. Greek ship. *Olympus* bound for Athens."

The reply from the submarine remained in German despite Dührer's feigned ignorance of the Teutonic tongue.

"*U-35* to *Nordsee*. This is an emergency. Acknowledge please."

The incisive command had the cutting edge of authority and Dührer hesitated. "Twinkletoes" Harper had once played the part of a Prussian officer in a play at Drury Lane and he had the character off to perfection. The submarine was now only four hundred yards off the tanker's beam and, approaching bows on, the German captain knew he was in direct line with the torpedo tubes.

"Slow ahead both," he told the quartermaster. He turned to Eckhardt. "Go and check the chart. See if there is a deep channel which we can follow in shore if we have to make a dash for it." He put the megaphone to his mouth again. "This is Greek neutral *Olympus*. What you want please?"

Hamilton was glad of the detailed brief Grenson had handed him with his sealed orders. If he had to bluff he preferred knowing at least some of the cards in his opponent's hand. He passed a reply to Harper who nodded and picked up the microphone of the loud-hailer again.

"Stop playing the fool, *Kapitan* Dührer. I have a sick man on board and I must get him back to Kiel without delay. BdU* ordered me to intercept you. You are to take him aboard. Stop engines and stand-by to transfer."

The submarine altered course to bring herself broadside onto the tanker and the two ships steamed parallel less than two cables apart. Dührer swore. It wasn't his job to play nursemaid to a U-boat. He was under the direct orders of *Grossadmiral* Raeder, not Karl Doenitz. But, like the majority of professional seamen, he found it difficult to refuse assistance to a fellow sailor in distress.

"Stop engines! Bring me alongside the U-boat, *Herr* Bootsmann." The tinkle of the telegraph echoed from the engine room in acknowledgement of the order and he looked up sharply as Eckhardt emerged from the chartroom. "Any deep channels?" he demanded shortly. If he couldn't vent his annoyance on the U-boat captain he could, at least, take it out on the mate.

Eckhardt shook his head. "No, *Herr Kapitan*. The only deep channel leads into Aadvaldt Fjord—and that's a dead end. You'll have to steer to seaward if you want to get away."

A green flare hissed up suddenly from the U-boat's conning-tower and, peering down over the side, Dührer heard a shouted curse followed by a sharp reprimand. The officer with the white cover to his uniform cap cupped his hands and shouted his apologies.

"Sorry, *Herr Kapitan*. One of these fools accidentally pulled the trigger of his signal pistol. No harm done. Can you drop a landing net over the side and we'll get our lad up as quickly as we can."

Dührer stared moodily over the side of the bridge and nodded his approval to Eckhardt. There was some-

* *Befehlshaber der Unterseeboote*=Commander-in-Chief, U-boats.

162

thing very odd about the U-boat now rubbing its rusty ballast tanks against the tanker's equally weatherworn beam but he couldn't put his finger on it.

*Nordsee*'s deckhands slung the landing net over the bulwarks while the rest of the tanker's crew leaned on the rails watching the transfer operation. One of the U-boatmen jumped on the net as it swung down and began clambering up the side of the tanker. Missing his handhold he slipped and nearly fell into the sea. His *"Donner und blitzen!"* sounded remarkably authentic as he clung to the ropes swaying like an inebriated monkey to the jeering shouts of the tanker crew.

Dührer watched the clumsy seaman. He could read the gold lettering on his cap band—*Deutsche Unterseeboots Flotille*. And he suddenly realized what had been puzzling him. Apart from the U-boat's skipper every other man on the bridge of the submarine was bareheaded!

He stared again with a new alertness. The officer's cap did not have the familiar high peaked crown of the *Kriegsmarine* pattern. And as a stiff breeze ruffled the duffle-coats he caught a glimpse of the English sailor's traditional square-rigged collar.

"Battle stations!" he shouted. "Cut the net lines! Get the guns on deck at the double. *It's a British submarine!*"

# CHAPTER TEN

"Open fire!"

Hamilton's reaction was immediate. Realizing his bluff had been called, he shouted the order before Harper had time to translate Dührer's sudden yell of alarm.

"Away boarders!"

Collis leapt for the netting, clawed his hands for a grip, and climbed toward the deck rails with the agility of a Barbary ape. Chief Petty Officer Blood and Joe Grainger followed with Warren and two other seamen close behind. Although the advantage of surprise had

163

given *Rapier*'s men the initiative there was little doubt that *Nordsee*'s disciplined crew would recover quickly and the men on the netting knew they had to reach the deck before the Germans could get their weapons into action.

Hamilton was staking everything on the apparently suicidal frontal attack led by Collis and Blood. No matter what the cost *Nordsee*'s defenders *had* to be diverted away from the port side of the tanker where Geoff Gilbert and his second boarding party were waiting in the dinghy.

The ugly black snout of a Schmeisser machine-gun poked menacingly above the edge of the bridge-screen as Collis hauled himself over the rails and turned to help Ernie Blood and the others up on to the deck. Hamilton spotted the danger, brought the rifle to his shoulder, sighted quickly, and squeezed the trigger. He heard a sharp short scream of pain and the machine-gun jerked toward the sky before sliding back behind the screen and vanishing.

A savage burst of machine-gun fire from somewhere high up on the tanker's poop tore Grainger from the netting and he fell back into the sea with a sullen splash. Bill Tropp, *Rapier*'s second coxswain, watched him drop and, crouching low behind the bullet-proof screen protecting the submarine's exposed bridge, he searched for the sniper responsible. He found him sheltering behind the starboard lifeboat and shot him down with the casual aplomb of a man potting china ducks in a fairground shooting booth.

Now that they had recovered from the initial shock of the British attack *Nordsee*'s crew were hitting back with merciless determination. Two more would-be boarders were cut down by a well-aimed burst of automatic weapon fire and, peering through the smoke and confusion, Hamilton saw that Collis and Blood were pinned down behind a large ventilator on the well-deck where they were exchanging fire with a group of enemy officers on the tanker's bridge.

Four more of *Rapier*'s men jumped for the blood-stained netting but an accurate burst of machine-gun fire forced them to stop halfway up the vertical side of the tanker's rusty hull where they flattened themselves against the plating as bullets whined around their heads.

"Up there, sir! Behind the charthouse!"

Hamilton looked up at the towering superstructure of the prison ship as he heard Tropp's warning. Eckhardt, *Nordsee*'s first officer, had found himself a strategic position on the starboard side of the charthouse where the overhang of the bridge wings protected him from the battery of rifles and machine-guns on *Rapier*'s conning-tower. He had four other men with him and their two heavy tripod-mounted machine-guns commanded both the well-deck of the tanker and the bridge of the submarine. Once Eckhardt had his miniature fortress in action *Rapier*'s valiant effort was doomed to disastrous and bloody failure.

Ducking down behind the bridge screen Hamilton wrenched open the drab green wooden box at his feet. He reached inside, took out a grenade, and crawled toward the rear of the submarine's bridge where the blood-red swastika ensign still fluttered in the breeze. Drawing the firing pin he stood up, swung his arm back, and hurled the grenade at the strongpoint. Seconds later the crash of the explosion shattered his ear drums and the charthouse erupted in an inferno of yellow flame.

"That's done the bastards, sir!"

Hamilton peered cautiously over the bridge screen. Smoke was pouring from a gaping hole behind *Nordsee*'s bridge. All that remained of Eckhardt's machine-gun emplacement was a splattering of wet blood at the base of the funnel where the body of one of the German sailors had been hurled against the unyielding steel like an overripe tomato thrown against a brick wall. Of Eckhard and the others nothing remained.

"Hold your fire, *Rapier*!"

Geoff Gilbert's head thrust into view over *Nordsee*'s starboard bridge screen. A discomfited *Kapitan* Dührer stood beside him with his arms raised high in the air. Hamilton seized the loud-hailer and held the microphone to his mouth.

"Cease fire, *Rapier*! Check! Check! Check!"

Looking up at the tanker's bullet-scarred bridge-works he saw that Collis had joined the others. The first lieutenant was grinning with triumph despite the blood streaming down his cheek from a flesh wound.

"Are the prisoners safe, Number One?"

"Yes, sir. The cox'n is below with one of the ship's officers unlocking the doors."

"Watch out for tricks," Hamilton warned. "You can't trust Fritz when he's cornered. We don't want anything going wrong at this stage."

"No chance, sir. It's all sewn up."

Hamilton holstered his Webley revolver and passed a hand across his face to wipe away the stress and strain of the last fifteen minutes. The moment of fatigue passed quickly.

"Right, lads, let's get cracking. Gilbert—take Blood with you and see to the prisoners. I want them embarked as quickly as possible. Collis! Round up a demolition party and sling every weapon you can find into the sea. Then go to the wireless room and smash the radio."

"Shall I disable the engines, sir?"

"No! We're here to rescue the prisoners not to destroy the ship. Remember we're in neutral waters. What's the casualty count?"

Collis consulted Leading Seaman Warren and Hamilton could see them checking the survivors. The first officer leaned over the bridge. "Five dead at least, sir," he reported. "Three wounded—Hopkins looks in bad shape. The dinghy's gone too."

Hamilton turned to Tropp who was busy cleaning his machine-gun. "Round up a stretcher party, Cox'n. And take the doc with you in case you need morphia."

"What about the bodies, sir?" Collis shouted as the petty officer hurried below to rustle up the sick berth attendant and a first aid party.

Hamilton shook his head regretfully. "They'll have to be left behind, Number One. Get one of your lads to check their identity discs so that we know who they are. That's all we'll have time for."

The lifeless bodies grotesquely sprawled on the blood-stained decks of the tanker were not, however, the full tally of *Rapier*'s losses. At least three men had been swept into the sea when the machine-guns raked the climbing nets. And until they called the roll Hamilton could not be certain how many men he had lost in the short savage battle to gain possession of *Nordsee*. He only hoped that the fruits of the operation merited the cost. But, knowing the politicians involved, he doubted it.

The liberated prisoners were beginning to come down the landing net and he hurried to the foredeck to meet them. They looked in a bad state—dirty, half starved and white as ghosts from three months' captivity locked inside the empty oil tanks below the water-line. Several of the men wore nothing but singlet and shorts although some of the more enterprising had managed to save their uniforms before abandoning ship. The agility with which they scrambled down the net showed they were seamen and, despite their ordeal, they were as cheerful as cockney sparows.

All, that is, except one. His fumbling awkwardness on the swaying net singled him out as a landsman. Bell, the wardroom steward, helped the man down to the deck and steadied him against the gentle rolling motion of the submarine. Hamilton stepped forward and grasped his arm.

"Professor Siberlitz?"

The man nodded and forced his gaunt face into a smile. His beard and stooped shoulders made him look older than his thirty-five years and there was a pathetic eagerness in the way he greeted *Rapier*'s commander. Too overcome with emotion to speak, he clasped Hamilton's neck and embraced him.

"You must be an important man, Professor," Hamilton told Siberlitz cheerfully as he disengaged himself with obvious embarrassment. "The navy laid on this operation solely in your honor."

"I do not understand." Siberlitz's accent was clearly middle-European. "I thought you were rescuing your own sailors, Captain. I am just a scientist. Who would want to save *me*?"

"Well, Churchill for one, Professor. I won't pretend to know what it's all about but you can take it from me, my orders were to get you off *Nordsee*. The other prisoners were only of secondary consideration."

Hamilton helped the scientist through the hatch and called on Bell to take over. "Put him in the wardroom," he instructed the steward. "And make sure he's comfortable. The others can make shift for themselves in the fore-ends mess space."

Working like Trojans the second coxswain's stretcher party had cleared the wounded from the tanker's deck and were just lifting the last casualty into the upper hatch by the time Hamilton returned to the bridge. Gilbert and his group were also safely aboard and, a few moments later, Collis and Chief Petty Officer Blood came down the netting having completed their work of destruction on the prison ship's deck gear and auxiliary machinery.

"Cut the lines, Number One!"

"All lines free, sir!"

"Half astern both." *Rapier* backed slowly away from the towering black sides of the tanker and, looking upwards, Hamilton saw *Kapitan* Dührer's face glowering down from the bridge wing and he couldn't help wondering what the prison ship's skipper would tell the Fuehrer on his return to Berlin. Enemy or not—he didn't envy him his task. Collis clambered up the side of the conning-tower to join the skipper. He kept watch ahead as the submarine reversed away from the tanker.

"Bows clear, sir."

"Stop port motor—slow ahead starboard. Starboard your helm, Finnegan." Hamilton watched the widening gap of water opening up between the two vessels as *Rapier* swung away. "Midships helm! Start port motor. Half ahead both." He turned to Watson who was standing just behind him on the bridge. "Tear that bloody pirate flag down, Yeoman. And hoist the White Ensign. This is a *British* submarine!"

*Rapier* was now well clear of the prison ship and white foam flecked back over the fore-casing as her bows pointed toward the open sea. The great adventure was over and Hamilton yawned as a strange lethargy replaced the tension of battle. Leaning over the voicepipe he called up the submarine's navigator.

"Lay off a course for home, Pilot. And send young Bonzo to the bridge," he added as an afterthought. "I'd like him to have a good look at *Nordsee* before we run behind Solvöe Head. It'll be something for him to remember when he gets old."

"Haven't you seen the casualty return, sir? Sub-Lieutenant Evans is missing. He was in the dinghy when the Germans machine-gunned it. We haven't seen him or Able Seaman Woodward since."

For God's sake! Not Bonzo!

Hamilton felt his body trembling as he closed the watertight cover of the voicepipe. Hunching over the bridge coaming he clasped his hands together and bowed his head as if in prayer. Poor little blighter— just a kid of nineteen. Full of enthusiasm on his first patrol. And he was dead.

For the first time Hamilton came face to face with the reality of *Rapier*'s casualty list. And he closed his eyes as a wave of nausea choked his throat. Bonzo and nine other men killed or missing. And for what? To save the skin of some unknown scientist who didn't even have an English name. What the hell was so important about Siberlitz that merited the lives of ten men? Grenson had said something about being an expert on nuclear fission. But what the devil was that, Hamilton asked himself. It meant nothing to him. And neither did Siberlitz. Perhaps that was what war was all about. Sending your friends to be killed to save the life of an unknown foreigner. And, on a bigger scale, wasn't that why England was now fighting Germany? To save a nation of total strangers in Poland?

"U-boat! Three miles on port bow!"

Hamilton dismissed the brooding thoughts from his mind as he heard the lookout's warning shout.

"Stand by to dive! All hands clear the bridge!" Swinging his legs into the hatch he jammed his thumb on the klaxon button as he pulled the upper hatch cover shut. "*Dive! Dive! Dive!*"

"Open main vents. Group up—full ahead both motors." Collis watched the big red needles of the depth gauges swing down and saw the bubble of the inclinometer move forward to mirror the angle of *Rapier*'s plunging bows. But she wasn't diving fast enough. A layer of salt water trapped by the cold currents surging from the melting ice of the fjords was holding the submarine awash despite her negative buoyancy. "Flood 1 and 2 compensating tanks. Flood Q."

The vents of the quick-diving tank in the bows hissed open as the Outside ERA spun the valve wheel in obedience to the first officer's instructions and, almost immediately, *Rapier*'s bows dipped sharply to increase the angle of dive. Hamilton slid down the ladder into the brightness of the control room.

"Level off at 30 feet, Number One."

"Thirty feet now, sir," Collis reported from the depth gauges. He glanced at the bubble of the inclinometer. "And diving!"

"Up helm fore planes!"

"Trimmed and level, sir."

"Up periscope. Attack team to stand by." Hamilton watched the phallic column rise from its greased womb beneath the deck. His philosophy of war was simple and uncomplicated. An eye for an eye. A tooth for a tooth. And the appearance of the U-boat had come like a gift from the gods—a sacrificial victim to avenge the terrible losses *Rapier* had suffered. Bending his eyes to the periscope he prepared to launch the weapons of vengeance against this symbol of an enemy he now found himself hating with a blind and uncharacteristic intensity.

"We haven't received the *Bloodhound* signal yet, sir," Collis reminded him quietly. "There is still a total embargo on all forms of attack."

"*Operation Manhunt* is over, Number One," Hamilton pointed out. "But they obviously cannot transmit the clearance signal because they don't know the prisoners are safe. And I cannot send my report until we are more than 100 miles clear of the Norwegian coast. In the circumstances, therefore, I propose to regard the *Bloodhound* code as received."

"Our orders were quite emphatic, sir. No attacks whatsoever until we actually receive the clearance signal."

Hamilton stood back from the periscope for a moment. "My orders are equally emphatic, Number One," he said quietly. "We attack."

"Very good, sir." There was no hint of reproach or resentment in the acknowledgement. Collis accepted the skipper's ultimate authority to do as he chose without question. Having said his piece Hamilton pushed his face into the soft rubber cups protecting the delicate viewing lenses and carefully examined the U-boat from end to end.

"Down periscope."

He looked puzzled as he stepped back. The U-boat skipper must have seen *Rapier* approaching. Yet he was making no effort to dive. It was almost as if he knew that any British ship he encountered in the area would be under orders not to attack. It was an odd situation all around. And Hamilton still hadn't found a plausible explanation of the radio signal warning him of *Nordsee*'s change of identity—or why the message had been transmitted on a German *Telefunken* wireless set.

Hamilton decided that the answers, if there were any, could wait. Right now he had an enemy submarine within range of his torpedoes and he was in a perfect position to sink her.

"Start the attack! Up periscope!"

The U-boat was still loitering on the surface. He could see the officers grouped in the conning-tower and the look-outs sweeping the horizon with their powerful Zeiss binoculars. The enemy certainly wasn't asleep. Yet although they must be aware of *Rapier*'s hidden presence they were taking no steps to protect themselves from the menace lurking just below the surface. Perhaps they assumed that the British submarine, with the prisoners aboard and with key members of its crew dead or wounded, would not risk an attack. Well, if that's what they thought, Hamilton decided grimly, they were in for an unpleasant shock. And settling himself comfortably behind the periscope he concentrated his entire attention on the task in hand.

"My range is *that*. Bearing of target *that*." Barrington read off the angles and passed them back to Gilbert at the torpedo director. The fruit machine whirred and clicked like a voracious gaming engine as he fed in the data. "Target moving directly across our bows. Speed 12 knots. Course . . . zero-two-zero. Down periscope!"

Hamilton's face showed no sign of the strain he was under as he watched the hands of the chronometer sweep round the dial. He waited exactly half a minute.

"Up periscope."

Bringing the lens into focus he observed the U-boat carefully to estimate its position, speed, and course. He would need at least one more periscope check to ensure the fruit machine had enough data but, with *Rapier* closing the range too quickly, time was running out.

"Half ahead both. Target maintaining 0-2-0. Speed increased to 14 knots." He passed the new range and bearings back to Gilbert and heard the clicking rasp of the settings. "Down periscope."

The final thirty-second interval dragged with infinite slowness and Hamilton had almost convinced himself that the chronometer had stopped. Except for the soft hum of machinery the control room was completely silent and the strain of waiting etched deeply into the gaunt faces of the men seated at the controls.

"Periscope—*up!*"

This was it! In thirty seconds anything could have happened. A well-handled U-boat could dive and vanish beneath the surface in half that time. And if *Rapier*'s questing periscope had been spotted, or the gentle whine of her motors been detected on the enemy's sensitive hydrophones, he had little doubt that the surface of the sea would be an empty void. Breathing a silent prayer to the patron saint of submariners he pushed his face against the eye-pieces.

*The U-boat was still there!*

"Group up—full ahead both motors. Target course remains 0-2-0. Speed 14 knots. My range is *that*." He paused while Barrington read off the angle and passed it back to Gilbert. "Bearing *that*." The artificer checked the scale and moved the celluloid window of his slide rule.

"Green One Five, sir."

"Got that, Geoff?"

"Yes, sir."

"Bring tubes to the ready. Down periscope."

Hamilton moved to the needle-slim attack 'scope with the unhurried calm of a man out for his evening stroll in the park. "What's her course, Pilot?"

Gilbert stared down at his machine. "Zero-two-two, sir."

"Director angle for an 85° track angle?"

"17° Red, sir."

Hamilton nodded imperceptibly. "Raise attack 'scope. Put me on director angle, Barrington."

The artificer rotated the column to bring the calibration of the annular scale into coincidence with the etched sighting mark on the brass ring.

"On director angle, sir."

"Stand by tubes . . ." Hamilton watched the bows of the U-boat slide across the field of view of the high magnification attack lens. In the cramped confines of the fore-ends torpedo compartment the torpedo gunners mate pulled the safety pins from the operating levers of the firing panel. "Prepare to fire . . ." Newton grasped the lever of No 1 tube. Only the skipper with his tiny glass window on the world above the surface knew the precise moment to fire and although it was the TGM's hand on the trigger he knew that he was no more than a humanoid cog in the machinery of death. If the torpedoes scored a hit any credit for *Rapier*'s success would be entirely Hamilton's.

"FIRE! One . . . two . . . three . . . four . . . five . . . six . . ."

Hamilton paused for a fraction of a second to give the torpedoes time to clear the tubes. Then he snapped the handles of the periscope upwards.

"Down periscope! Steer 1-8-0! Flood Q-tank! 80 feet!"

"Torpedoes running, sir," Baker reported from his listening post at the hydrophones.

"Steering 1-8-0, sir," Finnegan confirmed as he steadied *Rapier*'s helm on the new course.

"Sixty feet, sir . . . sixty-five . . . seventy . . . seventy-five . . ."

"Up-helm fore planes. Level off, Cox'n."

Hamilton watched the dials and nodded. "Nicely, Mister Collis," he acknowledged appreciatively. "Nicely."

He glanced at his watch. Elapsed time—20 seconds. He had fired at close range and the torpedoes should now be almost two-thirds of the way to their target. He began counting off the remaining seconds. Twenty-seven . . . twenty-eight . . . twenty-nine . . . thirty.

The reverberating concussion of the exploding warheads struck the steel sides of *Rapier*'s hull like hammer blows and she rolled with the pressure wave.

"Thirty feet!"

"Blow Q-tank, 'planes up!"

"Up periscope."

Hamilton swung the lens on to the last known bearing of the U-boat but the sea was empty. He moved the periscope slowly from left to right and thumb-flicked the high magnification search lens into position. A widening circle of oil scum scattered with splintered pieces of wreckage marked the final resting place of the enemy submarine. And, rolling sullenly like a repleted sea monster, the water belched with complacent satisfaction as bubbles of air vomited to the surface from the dying wreck spiralling slowly to the ocean bottom.

"Engine noises stopped, sir," the hydrophone operator reported. "I can hear sounds of vessel breaking up."

Hamilton nodded. He said nothing. For some strange and unaccountable reason he could not rid his mind of the U-boat that had come to the rescue of *Rapier* when she was helplessly grounded on the sandbank.

"For God's sake, Lieutenant. Why did you have to torpedo that damned U-boat?"

Grenson's patience was clearly running out. His phone had scarcely stopped ringing for the previous 24 hours and he was tired of being asked for explanations. And now that he had Hamilton in front of him he could work off his irritation on the man responsible.

"I thought we were at war with Germany, sir."

Hamilton felt equally short-tempered. The press had been waiting on the quayside and the newspapers were already headlining his exploits and dubbing him as "England's new Nelson." The adulation was not unexpected. The navy had achieved little in the way of spectacular victories in the early months of the war and the *Nordsee* incident had provided Fleet Street with a glorious opportunity of blowing the episode up into a morale-boosting story designed to keep the great British public happy. Hamilton did not allow the sudden fame to go to his head. He had the incident firmly in perspective and he knew only too well that the newspaper hero of today was often the scapegoat of tomorrow. "Perhaps," he added a trifle sarcastically, "we signed a peace treaty with Hitler while I was away."

"You're in quite enough trouble already, Lieutenant. Don't add impertinence to the list," Grenson snapped. "Your orders were quite clear. You were forbidden to take any offensive action against enemy shipping until you had received the clearance code word."

"I am fully prepared to admit I acted prematurely, sir. But I knew the code signal could not be issued until you had received my report that the mission had been successful. In the circumstances it seemed ludicrous to allow a sitting target—especially a U-boat—to escape."

"The first lord doesn't seem to think so. And neither does the DNI or their lordships." He sighed heavily at the memory of the telephone calls. But, having blown off steam, his temper was evaporating and he felt a little sorry for the young officer now facing him across the desk. "You did a first-class job rescuing those prisoners," he said placatingly. "Why did you have to spoil it by disobeying orders?"

"I thought we were supposed to use our initiative these days, sir. What would *you* have done in my place?"

"The same as you, I expect," Grenson admitted. He thrust his jaw forward aggressively. "But at least I'd have had the sense to have a plausible excuse ready when I reported to my flotilla commander."

Hamilton could see that Grenson's anger was directed more toward the authorities behind the scenes than at him personally. But, even so, he couldn't understand what the fuss was about. He had carried out his primary mission with considerable success and, as a bonus, he had sent one of Hitler's undersea wolves to the bottom. What was he supposed to do—come to the surface and shake the U-boat skipper by the hand? He swallowed back his anger.

"I'm sorry, sir, but I have no excuse. I've told you what happened and that's all there is to it."

"I'm afraid it isn't, Hamilton. Commander Mason is traveling down from London at this precise moment and he informs me that he wishes to see you privately. I gather he has a message for you from the War Cabinet. And to judge by the tone of his voice when I spoke to him on the phone—it's a raspberry!"

Hamilton shrugged.

"He's due here at 2:30," Grenson continued. "That gives you a couple of hours to sort out an excuse. Take my advice and have one ready. Now go and have some lunch. And be back here at 2:30 sharp."

"Very good, sir."

"And Hamilton . . ."

"Sir?"

"Speaking unofficially—my congratulations on a first-class job. Whatever the admiralty might say about your conduct you can take it from me, the navy's proud of you."

Despite his junior rank Mason had commandeered Grenson's office lock, stock, and barrel, and an armed Marine sentry standing outside the door ensured that no one would enter to disturb the interview. Hamilton looked at the commander warily. On the two previous occasions they had met he had sensed Mason's antagonism toward him. And he mentally girded his loins for the coming encounter.

"Please sit down, Lieutenant," the commander told him. "This is an informal meeting and strictly off the record." He leaned forward across the desk. "None of what I am about to tell you is to go outside these four walls."

"I understand, sir."

"No you don't, Lieutenant. But you soon will." Mason paused, helped himself to one of Grenson's cigarettes from the silver box alongside the telephone, and lit it. "I think I should tell you straight that you've been damned lucky. If Fleet Street hadn't heard about the *Nordsee* incident and turned you into a bloody national hero you'd be under arrest right now and waiting your court-martial."

"For sinking a U-boat, sir? It's an odd sort of a charge."

"No, Lieutenant. For sinking that *particular* U-boat." Mason drew on his cigarette as he thought ahead. He hoped he could handle the interview. It was going to be bloody difficult. But the first lord had insisted so it had to be done. He tapped the ash into a small brass tray on the desk. "I think I should explain that until this morning no one at the admiralty—not even the director of Naval Intelligence himself—knew any more about this matter than you did. The entire scheme was the brainchild of Section VI and I have been sent down to fill in the details. It seems that Section VI does not like doing its own dirty work."

Hamilton had no idea what Mason was talking about. Why the devil couldn't he start at the beginning instead of in the middle? And how the hell did Section VI come into the picture?

Mason had obviously read his thoughts. "Sorry, Hamilton," he apologized with unexpected politeness, "I'm probably confusing you. This will, I know, come as a shock, but Lieutenant Commander Cavendish's court-martial was engineered by Section VI. They knew all about his German contacts and, in addition, they were aware that the *Kriegsmarine* had a job waiting for him when the hue and cry had died down."

"Don't try and tell me Gerry was a traitor," Hamilton interrupted angrily. "I know he was always singing Hitler's praises but he was no Nazi . . ."

"Wait until I've finished, Lieutenant," Mason snapped. "Cavendish's pro-Nazi outbursts were all part of a carefully arranged façade. Section VI had been grooming him for his part in the scheme for a considerable time—several years, in fact, before the Kiel episode." He stubbed out his cigarette and lighted another immediately. "The mock attack on the German fleet was all part of Section VI's plan and they were gambling on a diplomatic protest from Berlin so that Cavendish could be court-martialed and dismissed from the navy. Your unexpected complaint to the c-in-c fitted their plans perfectly and turned what would have been a rigged trial into the real thing. And, well, you know what happened."

Hamilton nodded. He was never likely to forget. "But surely Gerry was killed in a motor racing accident last year. So how does he come into all this?"

"We were equally puzzled in the DNI's office. And remember we knew nothing of Section VI's scheme. We thought there was something fishy going on and that was why I asked those questions at the conference with Mabberly just before Christmas. We thought you knew something that we didn't."

"I can assure you, sir, I had no information."

"Yes, we know that now, Lieutenant. And I hope you will accept my apologies on behalf of the DNI for suspecting you." Commander Mason paused to collect his thoughts and then continued. "Cavendish's fake death was apparently arranged by the *Kriegsmarine* Intelligence Department so that he could officially disappear and then re-emerge as *Kapitanleutnant* von Hörst. The *Kreigsmarine*, you see, were equally anxious to keep the secret. Well, Section VI knew nothing of this and they nearly had fifty fits when they heard about the accident. They thought the Gestapo had discovered the scheme and had taken steps to kill him off in a plausible manner. It was six weeks before he managed to get a message back to Section VI reporting what had happened."

"But how did he do that, sir?"

"Fairly easily, I gather. One of his family was in the German diplomatic service and attached to their embassy in Stockholm. He acted as courier."

Hamilton was beginning to glimpse the end of Mason's story and he felt his hands trembling in anticipation. It all sounded too incredible to be true.

Yet, considered calmly, he could see the pieces locking neatly into place.

"Naturally Cavendish was posted into the U-boat service," Mason went on, "and it seems he made a big impression on Doenitz. But, equally naturally, he was always regarded with a certain amount of suspicion and, to prove his reliability, he offered to make use of his special knowledge of the inshore waters of the East Coast to attack our convoys."

Hamilton thought back to the wild chase through the sandbanks and shoals a few months earlier. No wonder he hadn't succeeded in catching the U-boat. A sudden doubt crossed his mind.

"But surely sir, that U-boat sank several of our merchant ships. I'm sure Cavendish would never have been party to murdering British seamen."

Mason shook his head regretfully. "Section VI were playing for the highest stakes, Lieutenant. Cavendish had to *prove* to his German masters that he was above suspicion. And in the view of the War Cabinet the information he would have access to in due course was of considerably greater value than the loss of a few merchant ships. The Intelligence departments don't fight the same sort of war we do, Hamilton. If eggs have to be broken to make the omelette they are quite prepared to break them."

"So that's why the U-boat surfaced to save *Rapier*." Hamilton derived no pleasure or satisfaction in proving the correctness of his original report to Captain Grenson. The end of the story was only too clear.

"Yes—and I suppose that's another apology we owe you, Lieutenant. No wonder Section VI did not seem surprised when we passed your report on to them." He paused again to light a third cigarette. "I need scarcely tell you that it was through Cavendish that we learned of the prison ships although, of course, we only received the information from Section VI without being aware of its source."

"So my radio operator was right. He insisted the signal had been sent by a *Telefunken* transmitter."

"The signal about *Nordsee*'s change of identity? Yes, it came from Cavendish's U-boat. And if he hadn't

179

taken the chance and used his own radio Dührer and his prison ship would have slipped through our fingers." Mason paused for a moment. "If it's any consolation, Hamilton, we know that the Gestapo also picked up that message. Cavendish signed his own death warrant when he used the U-boat's radio. Even if your torpedoes had missed he would have been a dead man the moment he set foot in Germany."

Hamilton remained silent as he digested the facts. It all seemed too impossible to believe. He grasped for the one connection with reality that he could remember.

"But you were talking about a court-martial when you started sir. I don't understand."

"I'm not surprised," Mason said sympathetically. "It was Section VI who wanted you busted. That single salvo of torpedoes from *Rapier*—fired in direct contravention of orders—destroyed more than six years of painstaking work. I'm not surprised they want your blood. Fortunately for you the admiralty take a more old-fashioned view of things. I don't think they approve of such damned un-English schemes. They believe in fighting the enemy fairly and squarely in open battle. It may not be the way to win wars but you have to respect their principles. When they discovered what Section VI had been up to they deliberately leaked the *Nordsee* incident to the press and made sure you were a national hero before you'd even got back to Harwich. And by doing so they prevented Section VI from going to the War Cabinet and demanding your court-martial."

Hamilton was still thinking about the U-boat. Although very few people would ever learn the truth he, at least, had the satisfaction of knowing that Gerry Cavendish had died for his country. And perhaps, by firing that fatal salvo of torpedoes, he had granted his friend a quick and honorable death and spared him from the horror of the Gestapo. In an attempt to hide his inner thoughts he seized on Mason's last remark.

"If the admiralty took all that trouble just to save me from a court-martial," he said lightly, "I must be more important than I realized."

Commander Mason looked up sharply.

"You're not," he told Hamilton grimly. "But the honor and reputation of the Royal Navy *is*. And don't you ever forget it!"

*Rapier*'s wardroom was completely deserted by the time Hamilton returned to the submarine and he dropped down on the leather couch with a weary sigh. Someone had left a copy of the evening newspaper on the table and he picked it up casually.

### NAVY HERO TO GET D.S.O.

*Lt. Nicholas Hamilton, the gallant commander of the submarine Rapier and the man who rescued a group of British prisoners in the face of German guns, is to be made a Member of the Distinguished Service Order the admiralty announced this afternoon . . .*

Hamilton stopped reading with a snort of disgust. Why, he asked himself bitterly, did they always give the medal to the wrong man? Why not Collis and Ernie Blood—they'd done more fighting than he had. And young Evans certainly deserved a posthumous award. The unfairness of the system only served to increase his gloom and he turned the page impatiently. His eye was drawn to an obscurely small paragraph squeezed into the bottom of the sheet and he paused to read it.

### DEATH OF A RACING DRIVER

*The Foreign Office has today confirmed the death of Gerald Cavendish, 28, who was reported as killed during a motor race in Sicily late last year.*

*(Reuters & AP.)*

So the big cover-up had begun. Section VI obviously did not believe in wasting time tidying up the details. A medal for the killer to buy his silence. And a lie to dishonor the *real* hero of the whole dirty business. As he

181

glanced down the page Hamilton wondered how many of the other news stories were the fabrication of British Intelligence. And how many other heroes rested unsung amongst the lies.

# More Bestselling
# War Books
# from Pinnacle
## Nonfiction

# More Bestselling
# War Books from Pinnacle

## Fiction